Brief FirsT EncounteR

Tom Miezejeski

Please Leave a Review

Reviews are the fuel of the publishing industry. Even a star review with a few sentences will be greatly appreciated. Reviews are the primary way that readers determine if they're going to purchase a book, especially self-published books. We also ask that you share your takeaways from this book with your friends, family, and associates. If you find this book interesting it should be interesting to your associates as well.

Prologue

The human species emerged about two million years ago, but only in the last hundred years has it been able to send radio waves beyond the surface of the Earth. Radio and TV signals are the only way that other civilizations might know that there is intelligent life on planet Earth. The first television transmission was made by Adolf Hitler at the 1938 Olympic Games. Since then, that signal has been traveling at the speed of light into the universe. Thus, knowledge of the existence of intelligent life on Earth is available to planets that are within eighty-five light years of planet Earth. While the distance this signal has traveled is huge in human terms it is only a small fraction of the distance even across our own galaxy.

The planets in the universe that could host life like humans, are distributed so widely that the chances of any advanced civilization detecting our signals are slim.

As Earth's signal spreads in ever widening circles the potential for the signal to be detected by intelligent life, that has developed the technology to find and decode our TV or radio signals, increases. But if that civilization has not developed technology that would allow communications faster than the speed of light, it would take another eighty-five years for Earth to receive a return signal. Even if that civilization was already prepared to send a return signal.

Planet Earth is 4 billion years old, but there are many other planets that are hundreds of millions or even a billion years older than planet Earth. Thus, if our signals are detected by another civilization. they most likely will be much further advanced than human society, at least in technology. It's more likely that we will be contacted by an advanced civilization before we detect one. This fictional work is a speculation about how that contact may take place and our reaction to it.

Permit me to observe that the term science fiction could appear to be an oxymoron, since science is about truth and fiction is fiction. On the other hand, science fiction allows us to speculate about what is in some other place or could be in some other time. In that sense science fiction is like science in that we develop a theory about what may be, that we later proved through experiment.

Science fiction stretches what our imagination can conceive, as limited as it may be. It's hard to believe that someone living even one hundred years ago would have anticipated personal computers or cell phones enabled by geo-positioning satellites. This work tries to call upon technology we are currently aware of or may develop some time soon.

Chapter One

The Earth Observatory was on the surface of the moon, but the most powerful telescopes on Earth could not see it because it was on the dark side. Mapping satellites could only see it when the dark side of the moon was facing the sun. Even then, the Earth Observatory was so small that it could hardly be detected by mapping satellites at the altitude they operate. Up close it looked like the rover Earth had landed on Mars. Except it was much larger. It had wheels designed to provide traction on an uneven surface and it had several mechanical arms that could possibly be used to take samples or make repairs to the rover. There were no markings on the outside and its gray color made it easy to blend in with the moonscape. On the top was what appeared to be an upside-down umbrella, probably a collapsible antenna and or solar panel.

The vehicle was parked between two outcroppings which would make it even more difficult to be seen from a satellite. There was a hatch that was large enough so that a person or a robot could pass from the interior to outside the rover. There were no footprints or tire marks around the vehicle which would indicate any recent activity. Some dust had accumulated on the vehicle which made it appear to be a shipwreck.

However, when entering the vehicle, it was obvious that it was alive and working. There were several panels that had indicator lights that were either steady, flashing, or dark. There were digital readouts in several places which would indicate the vehicle was at least partially operated by a live crew. If the vehicle was designed to be operated by a crew, the crew members must have been shorter than the average human since the headroom was only about 5 feet. Just audible, were the occasional sounds of servo motors that indicated there were some mechanical aspects to the vehicle.

On one wall of the space, which was most likely a control room, were two objects, which appeared to be robots. They had what appeared to be sensors that could detect light sound and other forms of energy. They also had appendages that could be used for movement and manipulation. They clearly were not space suits that would be used by some life form to work on the outside of the vehicle. The exterior of the robots had a very shiny finish. Possibly this finish was created to reflect solar radiation when the robot was outside the spacecraft in sunlight.

The Earth Observatory had launched a satellite into low Earth orbit to gather information about Earth. When radio silent it appeared to be just another one of the thousands of pieces of space junk that orbited Earth. When the satellite communicated with the home base it did it at a frequency and high rate of transmission that would make it appear to be just background noise to anyone tracking thousands of satellites circling the Earth. The observatory had been in operation for about 13 years.

There was a crew, but it was not located in the vehicle on the surface of the moon. Rather it operated in an exact replica of the probe located on the planet Cronin.

After years of research, Cronin society determined that it could get the flexibility of a live crew by having two matched vehicles but without the additional energy requirements of launching the crew and transporting them through interstellar space for long periods of time.

There was a permeant crew of 6. One was in command and Premier Ambassador, Gus. who was 60 years old in earth years which was only about halfway through a typical lifetime of about 130 years for people on Cronin. Thousands of years earlier the typical life span for Cronin was much shorter. Through good nutrition, exercise, and when necessary, the use of pharmaceuticals, life was extended to 130 years.

Gus made a lifetime commitment to being the commander of the Earth probe. Being commander of the Earth probe was a prodigious assignment. More prestigious than being an astronaut in the US space program. The population of Cronin was less than a billion. Thus, the commitment of spending on space exploration was a greater percent of GDP than in the US.

While Gus was the commander of the program on a full-time basis, especially after the probe reached the moon, at other times while the probe was in transit from Cronin to Earth he worked on other projects. There were intervals during the transit when Gus would be more involved if there was an opportunity to do a flyby of planets in a solar system that was nearby on the way. During flybys the probe could use sensors which could determine if life in any stage of development was present. Likewise, when activity was low on the probe other crew members also worked on other projects as appropriate.

Three other crewmembers processed the information as it was gathered. Another maintained all the equipment and finally there was a health officer that looked over the physical and psychological health of the crew. Duties were broadly defined so one member of the crew assisted another member as the workload varied. After being on station for about two years communication was in English. The daily routine on board followed the same sleeping and awake routine as a person living and working in NYC. The crew followed a five-day work week and even took two week vacations as long as the probe was manned by at least one person at all times.

The language and living protocol were set because it was believed that this made the interface with Earth Station better and would facilitate communication if contact was established. Once the probe got on station and started gathering significant amounts of information the support crew increased to hundreds as required.

While their physical appearance would never be mistaken for human it had many of the characteristics that humans have. They had two eyes, two ears and nose and mouth. They also had 2 limbs that appeared to be for locomotion and two limbs with digits that appeared to be used for manipulating objects in the environment. The most striking feature was the fact that they were covered in feathers. Not the course feathers. that you would find on a chicken but the nice smooth feathers you'd find on a Penguin. The colors were very dramatic, the captain was as red as a cardinal. One would have to assume that this species had evolved from some species like the dinosaurs on Earth.

Just as foreigners over the years had learned to speak the language of their adopted country, the crew watched television and movies. This activity also allowed the crew to understand the culture. At least the culture of life in the US as portrayed by the entertainment media. In addition to the media, a hack into the Internet provided a wealth of information about the Earth that could not be acquired by direct observation. It provided a very detailed history of the planet before the arrival of the probe.

Cronan society has been scanning the universe in search of life beyond their planet for over 3000 years. Life is defined as intelligent life that has reached the ability to use electromagnetic radiation for communication. Furthermore, radio waves used for communications are in a pattern that can distinguish them as generated by intelligent life rather than from natural sources.

.

About 1000 years into the search a series of energy pulses were recorded at time intervals and at energy levels that indicated that they were created by intelligent life either in warfare or some planetary engineering project. Based on the technology at the time it was estimated that the source of the energy pulses was about 75 light years from Cronin. Due to the laws of relativity and projected advances in technology to move matter faster than the speed of light, this incident indicated that the source of the energy was of limited threat to the Cronin civilization. On the other hand, it was decided that more attention would be directed to any intelligent life within 50 light years of Cronan. It was also decided that Cronin would attempt to minimize any contact with other intelligent life until a certain level of knowledge about the civilization could be acquired.

Using an earth calendar for reference, Cronan detected radio waves coming from Earth in 1945. They were radio waves that left Earth in 1910, which were the first few years of commercial radio on Earth. The radio broadcast of the "War of the Worlds" by Orsen Wells on October 30, 1938, reached Cronan in 1973. At the time they did not know what to make of the broadcast. Meanwhile, the program had evolved and improvements in technology made it practical to consider sending an exploratory mission to Earth to observe.

Originally it was thought that a manned mission to the moon would be required due to the complexity of the program and the ability of intelligent life to make any corrections unanticipated when the probe was launched. However, advances in their knowledge of how to use dark energy for communications swayed thinking in favor of the matched facilities. The elegance of the design of the matched pair was such that physical repairs could be made to the facility on the surface of the moon. Making physical repairs was one of the primary considerations for having a manned crew once this could be handled remotely, the weight of the crew and life support systems could be eliminated.

The best way to understand how this worked is to think about how drones are operated at a distance. Using input information such as visual and electronic data commands could be sent to the remote facility. While the use of dark energy allowed exceptionally fast communications between the two facilities the very large distance still resulted in some of a lag. Through extensive testing and experience it was determined what functions could operate autonomously on site. If a function was not anticipated at the time of launch this was done by making the changes on the physical facility in Cronin which would then be mirrored on the facility on the moon

Given the emergence of the Internet on Earth, this proved to be a fortunate decision. Over 90 percent of the knowledge gained about Earth could be read directly off the Internet. This capability combined with the raw data gathering capacity helped immensely with basic research.

Once the probe was launched toward Earth a discussion was started to determine a policy of if and how contact would be made with life on Earth. It was believed that Cronin may encounter some hostility out of fear, but due to a nonliving presence there would be no risk to Cronin society. However, Cronin may not be accepted with open arms. Decisions regarding how Earth would be contacted and what information would be shared would be made at the time of first contact.

After many years of learning from its mistakes Cronin society had developed a social order where there was limited separation between those at the higher levels of society and those at the lower levels. They had concluded that under circumstances of equal opportunity a person's achievements were more the result of a combination of physical and mental capabilities that were inherited rather than enhanced by significant. effort.

For example, Gus was the commander of the Earth probe mission mostly because most projects that involve several people, need to have a leader. A person was selected to be a leader just because a project needed a leader. The people led by the leader were equally capable of leading. This understanding of social order resulted in much less conflict. The leader had a more constrained ego than a person in a similar situation on Earth. Likewise, his subordinates had less problems accepting direction if they believed that they were receiving the direction just because someone had to be in charge, rather than the person providing the direction was in any way superior in mental capability or judgment.

Earth Station had a communication system that reported back to home base on Cronin. The system provided reports of various levels of detail on system telemetry and the information gathered from research. The system gathered information from sensors on the satellite, and from information gleaned from perusing the Internet. It even gathered information from time to time from several Facebook pages maintained by artificial intelligent bots. The system had the capacity to conduct focus groups on a wide range of topics just as major corporations run focus groups on consumer reaction to product features and functionality.

There were several levels of reports. The system compiled a summary of telemetry information and anything that would be considered breaking news was transmitted on an hourly basis. This report was compiled and transmitted via the dark energy communication system. Thus, in about two hours' time the crew on Cronin could have a real time monitoring system. This information was then added to the ongoing database of information that they had gathered over the life of the project.

A status meeting back in Cronin was held every day with a one-day leg. In other words, all the data received from the hourly reports the previous day was discussed. Every 30 days a more in-depth meeting was held to discuss trends in the data.

On Cronin today, the meeting was the regular daily meeting. The meeting was led by the probe commander and included representatives from the various disciplines working on the project. The task of making the report was delegated to one of his small group of people on a rotating basis. Thus, everyone on the team got a chance to interact with all people from various disciplines on the project.

Today the report was being made by George who headed up the computer systems part of the project.

"Good morning, everyone' he started to speak 'As usual we have a green light today." The system had three levels: green, yellow, and red. During the life of the program there had only been a few reports that reached the yellow level. There had not been any reports that reached the red level.

He continued "there have been some interesting developments. In the last few days, we have noticed a significant increase in seismic activity which would indicate that some major geological event is about to happen. The activity spiked significantly yesterday. Our analysis of the data tells us that a major volcanic eruption is most likely going to occur shortly. The exact size and location of the eruption has still to be determined. In fact, we may have to wait till it occurs to know it's location and severity."

Chapter Two

There were about 300 people in the Starlight Room of the Waldorf Astoria, seated at 30 tables accommodating 10 people each. They were donors and relatives of previous donors to the American Museum of Natural History, among the most important people in New York: businessmen, politicians, entertainers, and even a few from the military and the clergy. It was just a coincidence that the venue was named the Starlight Room.

The speaker, Neal Tyrone, was the Director of the Planetarium at the Museum. Neil was known for his ability to present scientific information in an understandable way. For example, instead of stating there are 200 billion trillion stars in the universe, he would illustrate it by saying, "Imagine a star is a grain of sand on the beach, then imagine that there are more stars in the universe than grains of sand on all the beaches in the world."

Neil was seated at a small table behind the podium, reviewing his notes. He looked up and watched the last few attendees file into the room, wondering to himself how the people in his audience would fare in another society where income and personal property were distributed more equitably.

A woman approached the podium and tapped the microphone to get everyone's attention. "Thank you for coming here tonight as donors to the American Museum of Natural History. I think our speaker needs no introduction. It is my great pleasure to introduce Neil Tyrone to you tonight. He is going to address the age-old question: Are we alone in the universe? And further, if there is other intelligent life in the universe, what are the prospects that we may ever contact another extraterrestrial intelligent society?"

After a brief round of applause, Neil began to speak.

"Thank you for coming tonight. It is a pleasure to talk to you about a topic that has always been my favorite. As you may know, the SETI project has been ongoing for almost

25 years, and we have yet to identify any indication that intelligent life exists anywhere other than on Earth. In recent years, we have discovered that many stars have planets orbiting around them, and some of these planets have environmental conditions that would be conducive to the evolution of life. Given the vast number of stars in the universe, there must be millions, if not more, planets like Earth. Based on this fact alone, I will say to you tonight that there is extraterrestrial life in the universe. Some of this life has not evolved to the level of sophistication to employ technology like we have here on Earth in the last 200 or 300 years, but there is a very likely probability that there are or have been societies that have evolved to have technology far superior to any technology we have developed so far.

"The parameters of the universe in terms of distance and time are many orders of magnitude greater than what humans think in terms of distance and time. Regarding the universe, age is measured in millions and billions of years, and distances are measured in terms of light-years, which is the distance that light travels in a year at 186,000 miles per second. Light travels almost 6 trillion miles in a year. As humans, we think of lifetimes of about 80 years, and recorded history is less than 10,000 years at this point.

"Fortunately, since light only travels at 186,000 miles per second, with the use of telescopes like the Webb Telescope, we can look back millions and billions of years into the development of the universe.

"While there are laws of physics that describe processes that appear to apply everywhere in the known universe, the processes do not occur at the same rate in the entire universe. As matter became more complex, it interacted with other forms of matter in different ways. For example, hydrogen is the most basic atom, which has one proton and one electron. Hydrogen is the fuel that powers the Sun. This process releases energy in the form of heat. Other stars that are more massive, with greater heat and pressure, can create other elements like oxygen and iron. It is said that we are made of star stuff because our bodies include iron, nitrogen, and many other complex atoms. Since these atoms are in our bodies and on Earth, it proves that the process of creating matter from energy is an uneven process. The iron that ended up on Earth had to be formed in some massive star at least 4 billion years ago when the Earth was forming from comets, asteroids, and other assorted materials which brought iron and other complex materials to Earth.

"While we may not know when conditions existed anywhere in the universe for life to start forming, it can safely be said that it could be a long time before it started on Earth. Life started and reached its current state about 1 billion years ago, or when the universe was already about 13 billion years old. Even if the universe had to evolve for 10 billion years before conditions were right for life to start developing anywhere, that was almost 3 billion years before we started our evolution on Earth.

"And with the geological record here on Earth, we can study the evolution of life over about 500 million years, which is about as far back as the fossil record goes.

"During those 500 million years, we have learned that there were five major extinction events, and we are in the midst of the sixth major extinction event. A major extinction event is when the number of species decreases significantly over relatively short periods of time. Probably the one that you will be most familiar with is the extinction of the dinosaurs 66 million years ago. The fossil record tells us that dinosaurs enjoyed the position of the dominant species on Earth for almost 200 million years. Only after their extinction was it possible for mammals to develop to the point that humans are now the dominant species on Earth.

"It is speculated that mass extinctions are caused by a variety of events. As you may know, the extinction of the dinosaurs was the result of the impact of an asteroid about 6 miles wide. Other causes of extinction could be massive volcanic activity or a supernova in the vicinity of a planet. The current mass extinction is most likely the result of the overuse of natural resources by humans. The most well-known cause is overuse of carbon-based fuels. It is projected that eventually, the Earth will be destroyed as it is enveloped by our star, the Sun, as it dies and becomes a red giant about 5 billion years in the future, expanding out beyond the orbit of the Earth. On a much, much shorter time frame, we live today under the threat of a global nuclear war that at a minimum could eliminate humans as the dominant species on Earth. The bottom line is that there are many causes that could lead to the extinction of extraterrestrial life, intelligent or otherwise. Even societies with vastly greater technology than we possess today could still be wiped out by a supernova.

"The reason I'm telling you all these things is simply to make the point that life, intelligent or otherwise, comes and goes at intervals that are far shorter than the time spans that we think of in terms of the evolution of the universe. If you think about the evolution of life in terms of astronomical time spans, an intelligent life form could be nothing more than a blinking light from beginning to end.

"Another way to think about it would be setting a date to meet someone at a restaurant. You arrive at 6:00, which was the time you understood to be the meeting time, on the other hand, your date thought you meant 7:00. You waited until 6:30, so you were already gone when your date showed up at 7:00. The fact that you did not meet doesn't mean that either you or your date do not exist; you simply did not make contact. Life could have existed in the universe, but the wide range of time when life could have started and ended in other parts of the universe could very well result in no overlap from one occurrence to the other."

Neil was speaking with the rhythm and intonation that would make one believe they were listening to an episode of Cosmos or some documentary on PBS. Neil reached over and pressed the button on a remote. "GOOD EVENING, NEIL. THIS IS CAPTAIN KIRK," came over the speaker system. Neil looked up with a startled look on his face, just like the rest of the people in the audience. After a few seconds, he smiled, and the audience laughed and broke into a round of applause. After a brief pause, Neil said, "you never know."

Neil resumed his presentation.

"The other factor that complicates or prevents the contact of one civilization with another is the fact that the universe is very spread out. While there are billions of trillions of stars in the universe, the stars that are 50 light-years from Earth number about 1800. Most of these stars are red dwarfs, which means that they could not support life as we know it. Within this 100 light-year sphere, there are fewer than 200 stars like the Sun which could support life if planets existed around them in the so-called Goldilocks zone, which is environmental conditions conducive to life.

"In summary, it's very likely that intelligent life exists somewhere else in the universe, but because of the separation of time and distance, it's highly unlikely that any two intelligent life forms have or will make contact with each other during their limited lifespan in terms of the age of the universe. One could say that the universe is a very lonely place for any one intelligent life form.

"When the astronauts traveled to the moon and took that classic picture called Earthrise of our planet, we got a sense of how we're all living together on a small little island in a vast, mostly empty universe. It's all we've got and there is very little possibility that we will be going someplace anywhere soon.

"I would like to add a positive note. If we should encounter other intelligent life, it most likely will be a positive experience contrary to what we see in most movies regarding contact with an extraterrestrial intelligence. I guess conflict is a central ingredient to movies so that's the way all of them project an encounter between Earth and extraterrestrial intelligence as a life-threatening experience where they take over the Earth for our resources or as a place to colonize. If you consider the intelligence that would be required to travel from some distant planet to Earth, that intelligent society would have the capacity to provide the resources required for its continued existence. They would not have to come to Earth for what we have.

"Furthermore, given the vast distances that separate planets, especially planets with intelligent life, it would not be practical to either take resources from Earth to their home planet or to move their population to Earth. To use an analogy, an extraterrestrial society that came to Earth for our resources or to colonize us would be equivalent to someone in Morocco traveling to Egypt for five gallons of water, even if they could do it using a jet plane. Due to Earth's gravity and the gravity of any other planet of similar size, it takes a great deal of energy just to escape the gravity of our planet.

"On the other hand, extraterrestrial society would have developed so much more technology than we have, and they would most likely be willing to share it with us since it would not be any loss for them or a threat from a defensive perspective.

"With that being said, I would like to add a cautionary note. Today, many things come with warnings; knowledge can be divided into two broad categories: the arts and sciences, which can lead to conflict. People tend to find themselves in one group or the other.

"Science has allowed intelligent life to have a greater and quicker influence on the environment than social change has allowed people to control the effects of technology. While science can extend the length of human life and improve daily quality, it can also create existential threats. In the past 100 years, science has enabled many more destructive wars and weapons than could cause the end of the human species. Even with efforts to improve the quality of life such as the use of fossil fuels for manufacturing, heating, and transportation, we are confronted with existential threats such as global warming, pollution, and overpopulation.

"Once intellectual life has let the genie of science out of the bottle, it is hard to control it and may result in the end of intelligent life on a planet. It could be said that science is like a disease once it gets control of its environment or host, it expands until it exhausts the resources of the host. Nothing can stop it until it leads to its own destruction. In the few short years that science has empowered the human species, it has already threatened its existence several times. Nuclear weapons are the first obvious threat. But there have been several others. There are less obvious threats such as the misuse of global information and communication systems such as the Internet. The current threat from the global pandemic has shown that society is not prepared to process new scientific information, at least in democratic forms of government. Vested interests such as religion, big business, and political parties will resist new information that is not supportive of their objectives.

"Based on the above, one can say that life has existed in the universe in any location for millions or billions of years, but individual societies came and go like the blinking lights on a Christmas tree.

"I'm not saying that we should not have programs to go to the moon and Mars and possibly colonize them someday. There will and has been many benefits to a space program; these benefits are enjoyed by us on Earth without ever leaving its surface.

"I would like to thank you for your kind attention tonight and look forward to meeting some of you on a one-to one basis."

Chapter Three

Neil liked to walk to work. His morning commute was ten blocks down Central Park West, into the park, and over to the Rose Space Center. This walk, combined with his evening stroll, gave him an opportunity to enjoy the outdoors and get in the exercise that other people might do at a gym. In addition, Neil was a native New Yorker, and walking came to him naturally.

While it's always been that way, New York City is a city of the future. The majority of people get to work by public transportation, powered by electricity. Even the last leg of most people's commute, the ride in the elevator to the floor where they work, is powered by electricity. Everyone, from corporate executives to entry-level administrative personnel, rides the same transportation system. In New York, at least in Manhattan, owning a car is an inconvenience. You struggle to find a free parking space, and in many cases, you have to pay a lot of money to use a parking facility.

Neil's assistant, Sierra, was already in the office, and she'd prepared coffee.

"Good morning, Sierra. How was your weekend?" Neil inquired.

"Just about like usual," she responded. "We had a birthday party for Peyton; he just turned 10."

"How was your weekend, Neil?"

"We went up to Connecticut to visit my daughter. The twins just celebrated their 4th birthday. It's amazing how time flies so quickly. We had a great time."

Neil carried a cup of coffee as he entered his office, walked over to his desk, and sat down at his computer. While it was booting up, he reflected on his presentation at the Waldorf Astoria a few days before. While he was the most qualified person to make the presentation, and the audience was very sophisticated, at some level, it reminded him of two people entering an elevator—one person says to the other, "How do you like this weather?" It was a topic that everyone could have an opinion on but had very little impact.

Neil liked to answer his own email. He felt that if someone had addressed it directly to him, he should be the one to review it. His email had already been filtered by many programs that eliminated spam and other unwanted communications. As he was reviewing the senders to spot any emails that needed immediate attention, a smile came to his face as he noticed one from Gus@earthstation.us. He thought that it must be from one of his friends or colleagues who was looking to have a little fun at his expense. Neil knew that NASA had a website named earthstation.com.

Meanwhile, the personnel on Earth Station were running algorithms that reviewed communications to find people who would be interested in extraterrestrial life. These algorithms worked the same way that the Defense Department used to find jihadists communicating on the

Internet. Neil was already on their list of possible contacts, but his name went to the top of the list because of the posting of the transcript of his presentation at the Waldorf Astoria.

The first contact with extraterrestrial life would most likely start with someone working for the SETI project and reviewing megabytes of data gathered by radio telescopes around the world, not from someone sending an email as an average Earthling would to a friend or colleague. "Yeah, right," he said. "Let's see how this goes." Neil knew that he had more important things to do, but his curiosity got the best of him, so he started to read.

"Dear Neil, I know that you are not expecting contact with another intelligent society to come in this format. But if you will let me, take a few minutes of your time. Hopefully, I will explain to you how this could be legitimate. I'm going to give you a way to find me. Attached to this email is a file with the topographical map of the area of the moon around our base. We assume that you have a military satellite that passes over our location on a regular basis. We will establish a radio beacon at 911 megahertz, and for physical verification, we will have three green lights on our facility.

We have been monitoring your planet for about 13 years. That is how I'm able to communicate with you in English using your technology. To convince you that I am legitimate, I'll share with you some scientific information, which you as an astrophysicist would appreciate.

In your scientific studies, you have determined that matter is composed of both light and dark matter, and astrophysicists have defined many properties of light matter by observation. But you can only speculate about dark matter because you have not been able to subject it to scientific analysis. Likewise, there is both energy and dark energy. I will try to present this in summary form and fill in some of the gaps with regard to dark matter, which you can later prove by analysis with which we can assist you. As you have already speculated, dark matter forms the infrastructure of the universe, with light matter existing on top of dark matter. A key characteristic of dark matter is that communications using dark energy are extremely rapid.

When we first started investigating, we believed that there was no time dimension in the dark matter world. This factor explains what you have defined as action at a distance and explains why gravity appears to be instantaneous throughout the universe and not traveling like light does in the light universe. Gravity is really the energy of dark matter influencing matter in the light domain. You've also speculated about what happens to matter when it goes into a black hole. Think of black holes as drains where matter in the light universe moves back into the dark universe."

The more that Neil read, the more he started to realize that this was not a hoax; it was the real thing. He found it harder and harder to focus on what he was reading. He found himself reading the words but not comprehending them. Rather, he was thinking of the consequences of what may be happening and how he would be involved with it. He continued to read.

"Before I go any further, it gives me great joy to share with you one of our scientific findings. I am sure that if our roles were reversed, you would feel the same way. After 13 years of observation, we have concluded that life on Earth is very similar or almost identical to life on Cronin if you adjust for environmental conditions and the timelines that are two planets have evolved on.

I know that we have both speculated that given the size of the universe and the number of planets that exist, it is very probable that life would have evolved on several different planets. However, until it could be scientifically proven, we could only speculate. I believe that during the last 13 years, we have performed one of the greatest scientific experiments of all time that proves that life evolves on separate isolated planets in the same way throughout the universe.

That being said, let me explain the purpose of my contact. Our society has been scanning the universe in search of life beyond our planet for over 3000 years, that is, life defined as intelligent life that has reached the ability to use electromagnetic communications. Radio waves have the only footprint that can be projected over the vast dimensions of the universe. Furthermore, radio waves used for telecommunications are in a pattern that can distinguish them as generated by intelligent life rather than from natural sources.

About 2000 years ago, this search revealed a series of energy pulses that were recorded at time intervals and at energy levels that indicated that they were created by intelligent life either in warfare or some planetary engineering project. Based on the technology at the time, it was estimated that the source of the energy pulses was about 75 light years from Cronin. Due to the laws of relativity and projected advances in technology to move matter, this incident indicated that the source of energy was a limited threat to Cronin civilization from any physical contact with that civilization.

On the other hand, it was decided that more attention would be directed to any intelligent life within 50 light years of Cronin and that Cronin would attempt to minimize any contact with other intelligent life until a certain level of knowledge about the civilization could be acquired. Using an Earth calendar for reference, Cronin detected radio waves coming from Earth in 1935. These were radio waves that left Earth in 1910, which were the first few years of commercial radio on Earth. The radio broadcast of War of the Worlds by Orson Welles on October 30th, 1938 reached Cronin in 1962. At the time, we did not know what to make of the broadcast. Meanwhile, the program had evolved and improved in technology that made it practical to consider sending an exploratory mission to observe the planet.

Given the time lags for communication and the complexity of the mission, we originally planned to send a manned mission to Earth. However, we discovered how to use dark energy for much more rapid communications between Cronin and our probe. Therefore, the manned mission was abandoned in favor of the system that we are now using to observe your planet.

Given the emergence of the Internet on Earth, this proved to be a fortunate decision. Over 70 percent of the knowledge gained about Earth could be read directly off your Internet, which helped immensely with basic research.

Once the probe was launched towards Earth, a discussion was started to determine a policy regarding if and how contact would be made. Since the project began 60 years ago to observe Earth, the Cronin society has encountered a crisis. It shortly will no longer exist due to an impact of a major asteroid.

We have a system that protects our planet from wandering asteroids that are on a collision course with us. The system has been in place for many years and worked well the one time about 1650 years ago when it had to be used. Recently, the tracking system detected an object that would have catastrophic consequences if its path was not altered. A rocket was launched towards the asteroid to perform a path change operation. Unfortunately, the rocket was hit by a much smaller object, one which was well below the threshold of the shield system, and it was destroyed. The small object was not tracked because the small object would have been burned up upon entering our planet's atmosphere; in fact, it was not even detected by the shield system due to its size. A backup rocket was launched, and it suffered some unknown failure.

We have a lifeboat system that allows a significant portion of our population to leave the planet in case of a major environmental failure or some other event that makes life on our planet difficult or impossible. Once the crisis passed, people could return to the planet and try to pick up at some point, even if it was at some place that was much more primitive than before. Our engineers calculated there will not even be a planet to return to. The energy of the collision will be so great the planet will totally fragment or even an explosion may occur.

After a meeting of the ruling council and a vote by all citizens, it was decided that the lifeboat system would be converted to a legacy arc. The contents of all museums and the contents of all libraries as well as all data processing and storage facilities have been transferred to the legacy arc. The ark was parked in an orbit about where Cronin exists, but at a safe distance from the exact location to be safe from the collision of Cronin with the asteroid.

We are contacting you to offer our knowledge base as a legacy of Cronin society. As you might guess, with over a 3000-year head start, we have developed technology well beyond what Earth has today. Just one technology that would have a significant impact on Earth is our development of fusion technology. Not only do we have the technology to do this, but we have also developed a technology that is much simpler than the approaches that you've been pursuing recently. You could call it cold fusion since we have been able to make fusion work at only 1000 degrees centigrade. We have determined that the use of catalysts in this process significantly reduces the energy requirement to get a fusion process to be net energy positive.

The ability to utilize this technology will give the United States a significant competitive advantage with the rest of the world while at the same time significantly reducing global warming. As you understand, replacing fossil fuels in the generation of electricity will significantly reduce CO_2 emissions.

Contact between two intelligent societies will have significant impact on the society with lesser technology. Therefore, the path you use to implement any new technology that we share with you would be very critical to success.

Since the technology that we will be sharing with you is a legacy of Cronin society, we ask that you implement any technology that you get from us in a way that provides the greatest benefit to human society as a whole. Many of your governments are organized along the concepts of competitive business, whereas a few societies especially the indigenous societies that existed in the North American continent before the arrival of European societies were a much more cooperative society.

It is well known to both of us that the laws of physics are the same throughout the universe. We have learned by extension that the laws of biochemistry and evolution through DNA are also universal throughout the universe. Therefore, many of the medications that we have developed should apply to you as well. We have developed pharmaceuticals that can cure or manage diseases such as Alzheimer's cancer and orthopedic diseases to mention a few.

When we transfer these pharmaceuticals to your society, we ask that they be produced and distributed along the lines of generic drugs rather than drugs that are sold and prices that recover their development costs. We feel that this is only just since the companies producing and distributing these pharmaceuticals did not have to bear the development costs which we have already paid.

Your society already provides certain goods and services on a communal basis, such as schools and highways. We would ask that when you implement our fusion technology that it also is implemented in a way that has the greatest benefit to all members of the human society.

We know that you have industries such as the natural resource industries especially petrochemicals and pharmaceutical companies that have a business model which is based upon a return on investment in research and development or infrastructure construction. These industries will be significantly impacted by our suggested process of distribution. Regarding pharmaceuticals, over the long term, this industry would eventually face the issues of slower growth and less profitability as the problems to be addressed diminish. When you take the very long perspective that we already have there's only so many things that can be addressed with pharmaceuticals. Regarding fusion technology, your society already briefly faced issues in this area. When fission technology was first developed you may recall some people said that the energy produced from fission technology would be too cheap to meter. We believe the development of this industry would be significantly different if it wasn't for the actions of the oil industry to suppress the development in favor of continued use of coal and gas in the production of electricity and certain applications of petroleum in transportation.

While you're reading this, I'm sure you're wondering what impact our contact is going to have on the general population when it is finally revealed. We wondered that ourselves. We started developing the probe that is currently on the moon decades before we first received signals from Earth that indicate it had intelligent life. Since we were developing the probe in advance of a specific target for the probe, we had to build in certain generic capabilities.

One of the primary reasons we developed the entire program that led to our contact was the concern for the potential threat of another intelligent civilization to Cronin. One of the things we had to determine was the psyche of the civilization that we are contacting. We needed to know if a society had an aggressive nature that would be a threat to Cronin. As a part of this overall capability, we also had the general capability of determining what impact our contact would have on the general social order. In other words, would our contact create chaos.

On Earth, as you know, many of the original fictional accounts of contact dealt with a physical contact with an aggressive society such as that portrayed in the War of the Worlds by H.G. Wells. These accounts were developed for entertainment purposes and may not represent reality. For example, many of your horror movies are designed to scare viewers even though they know that in the real world this probably does not exist.

In the last few decades, people on Earth have been exposed to various forms of technology. You started space travel when you went to the moon, created and launched a space station and its shuttle program to transport people and goods from the surface of the Earth to the space station. You have also made significant progress in microcomputer technology and cell phone communications. While most people that use and enjoy the benefits of this technology do not have any real understanding of the technology that makes this capability possible. They simply use it because it works. By the same token if people are told that there is contact with extraterrestrial life, they will be inclined to believe that it is possible. And that it may not be threatening; especially if there is no physical contact.

When our space probe was originally designed our intention was not to make any contact that would impact the daily life of the society, but we did provide for the contingency of contact if it became necessary.

As you know from your own space probes, the ability to gather information about a planet requires certain physical equipment to be present on the probe to gather the information and communicate it back to Earth. In the case of your probes, to take a picture of the rings of Saturn and communicate those pictures back to Earth, the probe had to have a camera designed into the probe before it left Earth. We had to incorporate certain physical capabilities into our probe in the eventuality that information needed to be gathered and communicated back to Cronin.

One of the capabilities that we designed into the probe that is currently on your moon was the ability to take surveys and at times anonymously interact with people on Earth to determine people's reactions, opinions and biases. While our probe was in transit, we kept track of technological developments on Earth. During the transit time from Cronin to Earth, which was about 44 years, we were limited by the speed of light to monitor developments as they appeared in the electronic communications on Earth.

When the probe left Cronin, it had to deal with the lag in our knowledge of your technological development. For example, in the early years, we assumed that we would gather information regarding human reaction to first contact by means such as e-mail. However, your technology has progressed rapidly to the point where you now have a worldwide Internet system with many capabilities.

Once we became aware that your Internet existed, we decided that it would be the most efficient way to gather information about your planet in general and to conduct surveys regarding human reactions to various events such as contact with extraterrestrial intelligence.

Just as you have software upgrades on Earth, we can adjust the basic capabilities of the probe to do research. We have been able to use dark energy to develop very rapid communications capabilities. Communications can now take place at 186,000 times the speed of light. Thus, while the probe traveled at only eight tenths the speed of light on its way to your planet, we could update it in a matter of hours using this new communications capability.

Once our probe was on the moon, we launched a low earth satellite around Earth which gathered information about your communication protocols. Which in turn allowed us to develop the software to gather physiological information about your species. For example, we created an Internet game called First Encounter which interacted with people on Earth as they experienced contact with extraterrestrial life. We studied their behavior interacting with this program anonymously, which hopefully eliminated any biases that may result if the people knew they were being surveyed. In other cases, we conducted what you would call focus groups to determine other information about human behavior in general.

Thus, we are confident that when people on Earth become aware that we have made contact chaos will not ensue. On the other hand, as with any change regardless of how it may come about, will cause certain changes in behavior, as people absorb the new information."

As Neil sat back in his chair, he thought, "This is going to be the most significant event in human history, and I get to be a part of it."

****

After a few minutes of thought, since he was an advisor to the President in the past regarding science and technology, the only obvious person to expand the contact would be the President of the United States and a small group of his administration. At least in the early stages, this would be a top-secret project.

After about an hour of thought, Neil put in a call to the President of the United States. He was surprised that he got a call back within about six hours; maybe it was because of his prior work with the previous administration.

"Neil, this is President John Adams, how have you been?" "I'm quite well, and how have you been?" "Well and learning what it's like to be a grandfather. They say that when you get to be a grandfather, you get payback for all the tribulations you went through raising kids as a parent."

"Mr. President, I hope you're sitting down. It appears that we have finally made contact with extraterrestrial life." "Well, Neil, tell me, how far away are they and how did you find them?" "Mr. President, they are right on our doorstep and have been observing us for 13 years. They actually contacted me. At the start, I thought it was just a hoax, but after careful consideration, it appears that it is true. I think there is a way that we can verify both for you and me that this contact is legitimate. They informed me that they were located on the dark side of the moon and provided a topographical map surrounding the area where they are located. I will forward that map to you. In addition, they said that they would be setting up a radio beacon at 911 MHz, which would have three small green lights on the facility. Mr. President, I think you will agree that this is a truly historic day and will have almost immediate consequences for everyone on Earth. Once you have verified that the base really exists on the moon, I look forward to meeting with you and your key advisors to plan our next steps. I look forward to meeting with you soon."

"Well, Neil, I'm in a state of shock. Today is one of those days when you don't believe what you're seeing but remember where you were for the rest of your life when you saw it. What you have told me is very believable. If two societies are going to make contact, it just makes sense that the one that's thousands of years advanced regarding technology will be the one to make the contact. Furthermore, while at first it might seem implausible that contact would be made via e-mail, but if you have a lot of technology at hand, it makes sense to me to use the technology that will get the best results.

I guess that I am the one that's going to have to sound a word of caution. Although it is very believable that we have been contacted by extraterrestrial intelligence, if this is a hoax, we are going to be very embarrassed when the truth comes out. Even worse, if this is some kind of Trojan horse, we must be on our guard. In either case, one could assume that only some other country that has advanced technology could perpetrate such a hoax or launch such a Trojan horse.

We must find a way to independently verify that the contact is truly from another extraterrestrial society. I suggest that we start by contacting the people over at the SETI project. If the contact is legitimate, we will accomplish two things. First, we will get the verification we require, and second, we would enable SETI to take credit for the detection of extraterrestrial intelligence. As they have agreed with their partners participating in the project, they would have the right to announce contact. This would take some pressure off for us to be making any kind of announcement until we are better prepared to do so. Also, it would be less threatening to society if they make an announcement of a finding of some extraterrestrial intelligence that is 35 light years away, rather than a contact from a probe on our own moon, which we have been told to be the case.

I suggest that you are a very logical person to make such a contact with the SETI people. I suggest that a good cover story would be that people in Defense were working on some top-secret project when they detected what they believed to be extraterrestrial intelligence. As I'm sure you know, the background radiation from The Big Bang was detected by two researchers at Bell Labs accidentally. At first, they thought they had some problem with their equipment until they realized what the source of the background noise really was. Even though they discovered this accidentally, they were awarded the Nobel Prize because they had the ability to determine what they were really seeing."

"Yes, Mr. President, that sounds like a good suggestion. Well, one would think that there are many stars that are 35 light years away. They really aren't that many, especially when you eliminate the stars such as red dwarfs that would not be able to provide the energy levels necessary to support life. Now that we have the Webb telescope in place, we can use it to do fine-tuned intensive research. It is my understanding that this telescope is focusing on regions of the universe that are far more distant than 35 light years away.

The only concern I have is that we were detected because of the leaking of electromagnetic information when we first developed television and radio. Some society that is so concerned about being threatened by another intelligent life form and has such advanced technology they may be able to hide themselves from any technology that we know of.

In any case, I will get on it right away. I know a few people over at SETI, and I'm sure they will listen to what I have to say and know that I'm not some crackpot investigating UFOs."

Chapter Four

The meeting was held in the White House Situation Room for two reasons: to take advantage of the audio-visual and communications equipment available, and to minimize attention on the attendees. Present at the meeting were the President, Vice President, Secretary of State, Secretary of Defense, Secretary of Energy, and Secretary of Human Services.

The president spoke first.

"Thank you for coming today. I want to start by saying, due to the sensitivity of what we are going to discuss, everything we talk about today should be top secret. We're going to discuss how best to handle the contact we recently had from extraterrestrial intelligence. Since their impact could be almost immediate and widespread, we must treat this with the utmost security.

Stated as simply as possible, we have been observed for the last 13 years by an extraterrestrial intelligent society through an observation base on the dark side of the moon. We have verified the existence of this observation base with one of our military satellites that scans the moon's surface daily. Here is a photo of that base." The president pointed to a screen at the front of the room.

"As crazy as it may sound, our contact was through an email to Neil. Rather than reiterate the details of this email, which are quite lengthy, you will each be provided with a transcript of this email when you leave today. Based on our interactions to date, it appears we are fortunate that these beings, for lack of a better term, have the best intentions for Earth. As you might expect, they possess much advanced technology that could substantially advance the position of the United States and the world over a very short period. However, as one would expect, some of this technology will be very disruptive to various sectors of our economy and the world economy.

Most of the work that has been done in anticipation of contact with extraterrestrial life has assumed that contact would be made via electromagnetic communications. As you may know, the SETI project has several   satellites searching for such communication. In addition, several protocols have been developed about how the contact would be handled internationally in terms of announcing the contact and how we would interact with potential extraterrestrial intelligence.

Since we have been contacted rather than discovering another extraterrestrial intelligence, I'm taking it upon myself to establish a protocol regarding this contact. Obviously, we are in uncharted territory and must adapt as we become more knowledgeable about this extraterrestrial life, the threats they pose, and the benefits they offer.

Since we must start somewhere, we will try to develop a general approach to absorbing new technology by discussing the implementation of fusion technology. I believe that while this is only one technology, it is one of the more important technologies with wide-ranging impacts. We have been researching this technology ourselves for several decades now, and we have made progress, but it's very slow. On the other hand, the impact of having almost limitless energy available without any of the negative consequences regarding global warming is worth the effort. Now that it's being handed to us, fully developed with engineering plans that could be implemented in just a few years.

This technology will eventually be the death knell for the coal industry and have significant impacts on railroads that transport coal. It will also impact oil and gas, not only domestically but also change the terms of international trade. As you know, we have been living with terms dictated by OPEC countries for many years. At least in these sectors, there will be significant demand for gas and petroleum to produce products such as plastics and fertilizers.

I know that there is a range of opinions on the role of government in these areas, but we do have a long history of regulation and allocation of natural resources such as oil drilling leases. In the electorate in general, there are many people who dislike government regulation or outright government participation in the market. However, the disruption that implementing fusion technology through a totally free market approach would be disastrous. I do believe that people will eventually come around to some government intervention. We do have recent experience with addressing the COVID-19 pandemic. You will all agree that if the government had not intervened significantly, the negative impacts of this pandemic would linger on today and for years in the future.

I know that you were not prepared for something of this magnitude when you came to this meeting, and I do ask that you go back to your offices and task your organizations to determine the best way to address this while at the same time keeping knowledge of this program as limited as possible. I think we could draw upon our experience with the Manhattan Project to guide us on how we can handle the security of this operation while benefiting from the experience of a wide range of people.

I am appointing the Vice President to head up a task force composed of yourselves and anyone else that he deems necessary to fulfill the objectives of this project.

Just as we have divided our history today between BC and the Common Era, I think history will be divided between before and after contact with extraterrestrial life. The impact will be that great. Before we end the meeting today, I would like to hear your initial thoughts on how we can proceed."

Neil spoke first. "Let me be the first to speak, Mr. President. I may be the person least affected by politics in this room, but even I have to modify my opinions and objectives to satisfy those who provide funding for my day-to-day activities. Everyone in this room, except for me, has a job that will only last as long as the current administration. If you want to be re-appointed, you're going to have to abide by the wishes of the voters who put you in office. Furthermore, it's an unfortunate fact of life today that major donors have disproportionate influence on the decisions of people who serve in government. Despite the long-term benefits of implementing fusion technology, voters in Texas who depend on their daily support from the oil industry will continue to support these businesses, despite the long-term benefits that can be achieved by implementing this technology, the least of which is a major reduction in the emissions of gases causing global warming.

We all have ideas about what is correct and most beneficial; unfortunately, these ideals must be tempered by the will of the majority. The skill of a true politician is finding a way to implement his or her ideals while also satisfying constituents enough to get re-elected. In business, they often use the expression the "salami approach." In case you're not familiar with that expression, it means that you can get someone to accept an idea if you serve it to them a slice at a time but would never get them to accept it if you present it to them with the whole salami at one time. In other words, our approach to how we present this challenge and opportunity will be crucial to how it is implemented and the final benefits that we accrue from it."

The Secretary of Energy spoke next. "I suggest that the success of implementing fusion technology will depend on allocating the revenues generated from this new technology, at the start, with programs that compensate individuals and companies who are displaced in an existing market. For example, we may be able to use revenues from government-run facilities such as the TVA program does now to compensate workers by eliminating the federal road tax on gasoline sales. I am sure that with good analysis, many other possibilities will be suggested, and some will eventually be implemented.

The transition away from fossil fuels to fusion energy will have significant employment impacts. Many people employed in exploration, extraction, and transportation from the well to the refinery, and then finally retail distribution will lose their jobs and will not transition into fusion technology even if their skills were appropriate. There are approximately 50 million people employed directly or indirectly by the petroleum and gas industry. A reduction of 20% in demand could result in the loss of 10 million jobs.

The introduction of new technology over the last 50 years has resulted in significant displacements of people in the labor force. For example, the telecommunications industry employed over 1,000,000 people as operators. As digital switches were introduced, almost all those jobs were eliminated. When people could not be transferred to other duties within the company, the telecom companies offered people early retirement or a significant reduction in force payments, which in some cases was more than a year's salary.

The major oil companies will have to develop similar programs as the reduction in labor requirements occurs. However, there will be some differences. In the telecommunications industry, the switch to digital switches was just a different way of doing the same thing. In the oil industry, there will be a significant reduction in activity. In addition to people, there will be significant assets employed in extraction, refining, and distribution which are no longer required.

If fusion technology was implemented as anticipated up until now rather than over 30 or 40 years, this transition could be handled gradually through the normal retirements and production facilities reaching the end of their normal life. Even in the past, these transitions have not been completely painless. The recession in the early '80s was primarily a result of the implementation of personal computers in the workplace."

The Secretary of Defense spoke next. "First, I would like to suggest that you transfer your email account to a secure server and that we set up one person in Homeland Security to have read-only access to your account. I know this will be an imposition on your privacy, but your email account is the only link we have in this matter, which has such significant consequences for everyone.

Since the beginning of the development of nuclear energy, the Defense Department has been a key player. At that time, the only use of nuclear energy was for offensive military operations. Since then, fission reactions have been devised for civilian applications. Due to concerns about accidents and disposal of spent fuel, development of this technology has been less than its potential. In recent years, due to the need to develop renewable energy, some interest is now being focused on renewed development of fission technology. For strategic reasons in the early days, the energy program was kept secret until we used the atom bomb in Japan. During the Cold War, other countries developed Atomic Energy for military applications, which eventually resulted in mutually assured destruction (MAD). There is significant precedent to develop nuclear energy within the Defense Department.

The Defense Department has used nuclear energy not covered by the controls that exist in the public sector. For example, we have nuclear-powered aircraft carriers and submarines, but none of these implementations needed a town meeting for approval. I believe that the development of fusion energy will have significant implications for national security beyond military applications.

In March of 1989, two professors at the University of Utah announced that they had developed a process called cold fusion. Rather than having a fusion reaction at high temperatures and pressures, they claimed they had developed a process that could involve fusion at room temperatures.

There are several takeaways from this experience. First, it gives us an indication of the reaction to super disruptive technology. While short-lived, the announcement of cold fusion had worldwide interest. And as would be expected, there were a lot of doubters that it could be true. While in this case, it can be assumed that the technology being offered to us will work. Given the time that they've had to develop the technology, it should be well beyond the sophistication of how we would have implemented fission technology.

In any case, we should attempt to implement this technology before making any significant announcements or policy decisions. I would suggest that we attempt the smallest scale possible implementation of the technology, because that should involve the shortest time frame from start to finish. There is the possibility that the overall process of a fusion energy generator is well known, but they may have used certain technologies in the process, that we have not yet developed.

While we are talking about the issues related to the transition to fusion technology, I do feel that I should mention some things about the Defense Department's role in the overall development of new technologies. The key to a strong National Defense and maintaining our position as a world leader has resulted from the implementation of new technologies such as global positioning satellites.

While our new benefactors have asked that we share the technologies that they will give us with other countries, we must still try to maintain our technical superiority. If that is not possible, I think we must rely upon our experience in relationships that we have developed over the last decades for arms control. I am optimistic that this is possible when countries came to the realization had nothing could be gained using such destructive technologies as the atom bomb, they realized that the only alternative was to negotiate that they're not used by anyone. In that same spirit, we will have to develop agreements that any technology we receive from our extraterrestrial neighbors will not be distributed or used anyway that allows any one country to use it aggressively against another country."

The Secretary of State spoke next.

Mr. President, we are on uncharted grounds regarding this matter. Under the concepts of national sovereignty, each country is allowed to develop the natural resources that are within their boundaries. Even regarding nuclear energy, which is implemented in the civilian sector, it is done under significant licensing controls. Also, under patent law, new technology can be patented. The developer has the right to generate revenue from the sale or implementation of that technology.

We cannot really say that the fusion technology that we would get from our new neighbors is a national resource that is exclusively ours to exploit. Most of the international agreements that exist today, such as NATO and the UN, were established to provide for defense or address negative situations such as COVID-19 or global warming. While the UN has many aid programs, none of them would be on the scale of sharing fusion technology. In centuries past, when one society met another, such as when Europeans visited the Americas, the Europeans exploited the indigenous populations. In our current situation, this would be the opposite. We would be sharing our national wealth with developing countries. Whether we were contacted by extraterrestrial intelligence, we would eventually reach a point where our technology would allow for enough abundance that scarcity of resources would no longer be an issue for people or countries.

The United States has always prided itself on helping other countries in need and has tried to be a model of democratic government governed by ethics. There is no question that we have at times exploited our position of strength. However, we are living in a world where other countries have a similar ability. For example, the OPEC countries can control the price of oil and thus the revenue they generate from their natural resources. Specifically in this regard, fusion energy would be very disruptive, and the natural resources that appeared to be like money in the bank for these countries would now be significantly devalued. Even within our own borders, our efforts to control global warming have been hindered in one way or another by interests that want to preserve the value of their resources and the revenue streams that come from them.

Unlike any of the aid programs we now have with other countries where we share resources and assets developed by our efforts in the United States, we are the custodian of the technology entrusted to us by our extraterrestrial benefactors."

Finally, the Secretary of Human Services spoke.

"Mr. President, I hate to be the one to speak a word of caution regarding our presumed good fortune to receive technology from the people of Cronin. However, I would like to spend a few minutes talking about some different points of view regarding the use of technology.

There was an English gentleman who was both an author and a scientist. His name is C.P. Snow, and he lived from 1905 until 1980. He had an unusual background. His formal education was in science, specifically chemistry. However, most of his working career was devoted to being an author. This unique experience allowed him to travel in the circles of both scientists and, as they were called at the time, intellectuals. These so-called intellectuals could also be characterized as non-scientists.

Having interacted with scientists in one part of the day and non-scientists in another part of the day, he came to the realization that these two groups very seldom interacted with each other. Most likely, this was because there was a lack of a detailed understanding of what the other group did daily. He further observed that the nature of their work caused them to have a different approach to social issues. Scientists engaged in activities that were forward-thinking, and they perceived change to be a positive thing. On the other hand, the intellectuals were concerned with preserving social standards which complied with the established order of things. Being that he was in English society, he further observed that these two groups pursued their objectives more rigorously than people in other societies.

This difference in approach to progress resulted in a gap between the social behavior of scientists and intellectuals, with the intellectuals lagging the scientists. Some people might characterize this difference as a shortcoming of intellectuals, as they had to catch up in their thinking with the things that were being presented daily by scientists. It is my belief that 50 years later, this gap has become even wider as science has become more advanced and specialized. Scientific knowledge has expanded so rapidly that it is no longer possible for a generalist to stay informed enough for any one of the specialties to be a productive participant in that branch of science.

He also expressed the belief that technology resulted in a gap between the rich and poor, whether it be individuals, companies, or entire nations. He expressed the belief that technology was a form of capital which allowed people in societies to generate income and wealth using the advantage that they had through technology. This advantage allowed richer individuals to widen the gap between them and the poor. The rich got richer, but the poor got poorer, or at best maintained their status without improvement.

If you look at our experience with efforts to control global warming, this, in fact, is true. Whenever nations have gotten together and established goals and standards regarding CO_2 emissions, the poorer countries have expressed their frustration. Why should they now be asked to limit their production of greenhouse gases while the advanced economies have already exploited these resources to become wealthy?

Within our own society, the gap between scientists and non-scientists is causing frustration and controversy. It is easy to assume that individuals and groups who are against measures to limit the emission of greenhouse gases are simply the result of one group trying to protect their economic position. There is no question that there will be winners and losers in our efforts to control global warming. Producers in the fossil fuel industry will definitely see a decline in the demand for their products, and there has been documentation by some of the actors in this industry to frustrate true science with regard to global warming.

On the other hand, there is a significant gap in the understanding of scientists and non-scientists regarding global warming. Scientists are aware of studies of ice cores and other ways of learning about the CO_2 cycle on Earth in other times that can be used as an indicator of the challenge we face regarding global warming. In other words, among scientists, there is very little question that we have a problem. Meanwhile, non-scientists who do not understand how science takes place are led to believe by some other information source that there is not a problem or at least that it is not as great as being projected by the scientific community.

I would also like to briefly discuss the process by which technology is implemented. It is amazing how often technology was implemented and had social impacts far beyond what was originally anticipated. We are all aware of the significant role that Facebook has in our society. This technology was originally developed simply to allow college students to communicate with each other. As we all know, over time the user community expanded from a limited group of college students to almost every member of society today. Furthermore, no one anticipated the economic and social impact that this technology would have on our society. Entrepreneurs realized that having access to large numbers of people and influencing them for their economic benefit, many times without Facebook users knowing they were being influenced by the practices of these entrepreneurs.

As we also know, other people with political agendas used this technology to influence people. In this country, the press has traditionally been a check on the activities of politicians and corporations by making people aware of facts regarding their activities. The traditional media had controls that allowed citizens to rely on the information that they read or saw in the media. In the interest of a free marketplace and making technology available to everyone, the Internet was not subject to similar controls. We are all aware of the abuses of some actors to use this technology for their benefit rather than the benefit of society.

With all this being said, its obvious politics is having a big impact on people trying to control the effect technology is having on the environment. Fortunately, the negative impact of the misunderstanding of technology has been limited by the rate at which new technology can be discovered and implemented. If we are all presented with a large amount of new technology all at one time, our society could be overwhelmed in several ways.

The fossil fuel industry was the major factor in developing all the goods and services that we enjoy today from the industrial revolution. The Industrial Revolution changed the way all people lived. People who lived on farms moved into the cities and in many ways suffered a decline in their quality of life. At the same time, the industrial revolution allowed a significant transfer of wealth from one part of society to another. I will admit that society today is much better off than it was before the industrial revolution.

The fossil fuel industry had a great impact because it replaced the work that people and animals could perform with machinery powered by fossil fuels or electricity generated using fossil fuels.

Today we have learned that the use of these fossil fuels upsets the balance of nature. Humans have impacted the Earth's environment over the last 200 years as much as natural change has over 20,000 years.

Thank you for allowing me to express caution regarding what on the surface might appear to be a blessing from technology from the Cronin people."

The president concluded the meeting by asking everyone to reconvene in three days at 4:00 in the afternoon. "Please feel free to bring any experts that you think would help".

Chapter Five

Neil sat down in front of his computer, and as it was booting up, he thought to himself, "I'm sure that email was used to facilitate the communications between Earth and Cronin." In other words, people on Cronin may not even communicate via the spoken word but may use some kind of system of clicks and songs used by birds and other animals on Earth. Neil further thought, that while email facilitated communications with some unknown translation taking place, it also allowed asynchronous communications: I write to Gus, and Gus writes back with some time lag between.

Neil began to write.

"I'd like to give you an update on how things are proceeding on my end here. I have contacted the President of the United States, and he has formed a working task force to determine the best way to exchange information between ourselves. As we both know, the exchange of technology, most of it coming from you to us, will have a great social impact on Earth society. As a trial run of developing this procedure, we have decided to see how we would implement fusion technology. You mentioned in your prior communication that your society had long ago developed the technology to use fusion as a source of energy. It would be greatly helpful to us in this project if you have an engineering document that describes the physical characteristics of the generating facility and how it is controlled and implemented. We can then use this information to see how our existing energy generation systems would be impacted, if we implemented fusion technology. Since you've had experience implementing a typical fusion reactor, it would be helpful if you could provide a typical timeline for implementing such a project. As always, the first pass at anything has its unexpected problems which are overcome eventually but lengthen the total implementation project. Once you've done it a few times, the time required to implement it will be much less than the first effort. Thus, if you could provide files via return email that provide the engineering documents and a timeline, it would be very helpful. Thank you so much for this information. We are also exploring what we refer to as cold fusion. This fusion process involves a chemical type of reaction assisted by a catalyst such as palladium. If you have any experience with this process, we would like to know if it has been implemented and how. As the director of the Rose Space Center at the American Museum of Natural History, I'm interested to learn what you can tell me about your space program currently and how it has progressed. Since you have been in the process of scientific discovery for about 3000 years longer than we have, I'm interested to know what you have learned about the overall process. I am also interested in your experience with aggressive behavior in intellectual beings. Over the 5000 years of recorded history in our society, it appears that aggressive behavior has always been present and based on our current situation, it still is. I assume that this behavior might be a part of what we call survival of the fittest. I would assume that evolution is a universal phenomenon. Otherwise, we wouldn't be speaking today. Your society must have evolved from some lesser level of intelligence at some time in the past. Part of our understanding of survival of the fittest is that species or individuals that are best adapted to the current environment survive and then pass these capabilities to the next generation through their DNA. Thus, the species or individual that has some characteristic that makes it more survivable in the current environment wins out over a lesser qualified individual. As you may know, humans, which are mammals, only evolved to our status after the dinosaurs were wiped out by the impact of an asteroid 65 million years ago. Over a shorter time, homo sapiens coexisted with Neanderthal man for some time before Neanderthal man went extinct. Since your society has about 3000 more years' experience with evolution and social behavior, I am wondering if you have found a way to channel aggressive behavior so that it leads to better outcomes. I am sure you will agree that aggressive behavior combined with advanced technology can be very counterproductive and even threaten the existence of a species. For the time being, it seems that we on Earth have controlled the potential species-threatening behavior of nuclear warfare through arms control agreements. I look forward to hearing back from you as soon as possible. Thank you".

Two days later, Neil received the following email:

"Your request for information about how we implement fusion technology raises an issue that we should discuss at this time about the overall process of technology transfer. As you would expect, transferring our technology to you will have a great impact on scientific research already taking place on Earth. Furthermore, I would like to point out something which you may have also thought about: the impact of us transferring technology to you that is currently in development in various organizations on Earth.

If we can provide you with technology information which will solve things that you are currently researching, the most logical thing for your researchers to do is suspend their efforts. There are some good news and bad news aspects to this issue. The bad news regarding this transfer is that people who are currently engaged in high-paying jobs doing this research might be unemployed. The good news is, in many cases, we can't just simply hand over documents that describe our new technology. As with the technology that you have already developed on Earth, you know that once the technology is developed, it must be disseminated to other people who will be involved in implementing it.

For lack of a better term, we could call these people engineers. You will be required to significantly refocus the assets in your university system from basic research to teaching to implement the dissemination of the new technology. In many cases, technology is an incremental development process where one process is used to develop another process. We have several technologies where our learning has progressed to the point where we are two iterative steps ahead of you regarding basic science. Therefore, before some of these technologies can be implemented, we will have to backfill through training the experience and knowledge base of the prior iterative steps in the development process that you have not reached in your own technology development to date.

Specifically, regarding fusion technology, we believe that you have the basic scientific information and technology that will allow you to implement this without much reeducation. I would also like to raise another issue regarding technological development. In some cases, the basic technology developed does not have negative consequences, but when used in extremes may result in negative consequences.

The best example that I can give is what your current experience has been regarding development in the petrochemical industry, which has led to global warming. If the population of Earth were significantly less, the Earth's environment would be able to tolerate this technology to some degree. We have learned that there are limits to how much technology can be implemented relative to the population on a planet. Today you have approximately 8 billion people on planet Earth. There is a wide variation in the degree of economic development from country to country. If everyone on the planet were brought up to the economic level of the highest-income groups, the materials and other resources required to accomplish this task would be more than those available on your planet.

We have learned that you are already implementing some programs to address this issue. They are generally categorized as sustainability. Sustainability will be the ultimate requirement to implement all the technologies that we can transfer to you. Finally, some technologies can have significant negative effects if placed in the hands of the wrong people, either individuals or entire countries. You have made efforts to address this issue with your nuclear arms agreements. However, it appears that somehow you have not controlled the access of military weapons to people who are qualified to use them.

Neil, I would also be very happy to share with you information about our space exploration program. I'd like to give you two facts which would give you an understanding about our philosophy on space exploration. We have learned by using dark energy it is possible to communicate at 186,000 times faster than the speed of light. That's so fast that at the time that we discovered it, we had no way to measure it, so we started to assume that in the world of dark matter and energy there was no time dimension. So far, we have only been able to move matter at about 80% of the speed of light. Our planet is located about 35 light years from yours. While it took almost 44 years for our space probe to reach your moon, we can communicate with it via dark energy with a transit time of about one hour and 40 minutes.

As you can see, interstellar exploration has limits regarding moving physical probes. Once the probe is in place, we can communicate with it in a short period of time. Furthermore, we have eliminated the use of manned probes, since our technology has advanced to the point where we can provide most of the redundancies that are necessary to assume that the probe will be operational throughout its entire journey to its intended location. When our planned redundancies have failed, we can attempt a fix via communications that only takes an hour and 40 minutes.

Furthermore, we have been able to develop robotic technology which can duplicate most of the physical capabilities of a live crew member. The probe located on your moon has two of these robots that can be activated to make repairs where physical activity is required. The use of manned space probes also significantly impacts the size of the probe. In addition to the weight of the crew you have all the additional equipment and fuel that's required to maintain life on the spacecraft. During long transit periods such as to your moon, the spacecraft can be put to sleep with very little energy requirements.

Also, a living crew cannot withstand the extreme conditions of space travel such as the acceleration and deceleration for the start and end arrival at the intended location. The above limitations have had further implications on our philosophy regarding space exploration. Simply stated, our primary objective is to gather information about other intelligent life and to share information with that intelligent life as we are doing with you.

Since we have advances in technology that allow us to provide for our various needs locally, we do not have to travel to another planet for natural resources or for colonization. As I told you earlier, our planet faces the unusual event of extinction due to collision with an asteroid. Even with all the technology that we have, there is no practical way to evacuate even a small portion of our society to another planet that has conditions that would permit life as we have it now. The probe that we sent to your moon only weighs about 10 tons which is only a small fraction of the size of a manned spacecraft if we wanted to ask the crew to endure 44 years of travel to get to their destination.

We have decided that manned spacecraft and travel is only practical within our own solar system. Unfortunately, our planet is the only planet that exists in what you refer to as the Goldilocks zone. Thus, we have nowhere to escape to. When you compare our ratio of the time to move matter with the speed of communication to your capabilities of moving matter and communications within your own solar system, it only seems practical for movement within your own solar system.

Over time we may develop the technology to move matter more rapidly and comparable to the speed of communications and other intelligent life may also develop this capability we still cannot see a cost benefit to manned space exploration. Regarding your other question about aggressive behavior being built into human DNA. I agree that your assessment is correct regarding it being a part of survival of the fittest. However, we have learned that other behaviors, such as a preference for sweets and fats, are also built into DNA. We have learned that the key to controlling these negative behaviors is recognizing that they exist and having educational programs that make individuals aware at an early age that they exist and how to channel behavior into positive results rather than negative behaviors such as warfare.

As you mentioned we do have 3000 more years of experience with technology. Somewhere along our progression in these three thousand years, we realized that greater attention must be placed on constructive social behavior rather than just harnessing the physical powers of the universe to make life better. I thought it would be helpful if I gave you some background information on our efforts to identify other plants that contain intelligent life, at least planets that have acquired the technology to transmit radio energy which can be detected from a distance.

Our program to detect societies using these criteria has been in place for well over 3000 years on Cronin. The program has the capacity to detect radio waves originating from planets within 100 light-years of Cronin. As you may know, the energy level of these radio waves is quite small relative to the energy levels that can be released by celestial bodies. During this time, we have only detected 5 planets emanating radio waves besides planet Earth. Of these five instances, two were already broadcasting when our system came online. Thus, we have no way of knowing how long they were emitting radio waves before we were able to detect them. Of these two, one stopped transmitting information about 900 years after it was discovered, the other continues to transmit data today. In addition, the other three signals came online after our system was in place. One signal was detected about 1100 years ago and the other was detected 1300 years ago. The signal that we detected 1100 years ago stopped abruptly about 200 years ago. We can only assume that this planet encountered some geological or astronomical event that caused the abrupt cessation of radio transmission. The signal that was detected 1300 years ago stopped gradually over 10 years, about 800 years ago. We can only assume that this pattern of declining radio transmissions indicated some other factors that resulted in the decline of the society creating the radio transmission. Finally, we detected the final transmission about 150 years ago. In all cases, we were only able to simply identify that the signals appear to be from intelligent life. It was not possible for us to decode the information that was being broadcast over that signal. As you know, Cronin will abruptly stop radio transmission once it is impacted shortly by the asteroid. Our overall scientific conclusion from this experience makes us believe that the life of intelligent societies is relatively short compared to astronomical time spans of stars, planets, and other inanimate objects in the universe. One could also say that technology does not seem to work well toward continuing intelligent life.

When we launched our probe towards planet Earth over 50 years ago, it was our first attempt to make contact with another intelligent society. We did not know what to expect when the probe arrived in the vicinity of your planet. Therefore, we incorporated as much technology for information gathering as we anticipated could be used and then provided for the ability to provide updates once the probe got on station.

Earth was the only planet that was close enough to make it practical to launch a probe like the one that we put on your moon. Over the 13 years that we have been observing planet Earth, we have acquired a significant amount of information about life today on planet Earth and the history of your planet that has been discovered by archaeologists, paleontologists, and other scientists that can study the fossil record. This told us about the evolution of various life forms until intelligent life emerged and then used recorded information to get an even more detailed history of your planet. We compared this information with information that we have regarding the evolution of life on planet Cronin. It is amazing how similar this evolutionary process was on two planets separated by 35 light-years.

Having access to information about the history of your planet before you were able to transmit radio information allowed us to come to a few conclusions. As you know, the Roman Empire spanned a period of approximately 1000 years. It increased its dominance over other societies on Earth for about 500 years, remained at that level of dominance for about 200 years, and declined for about 300 years.

To understand the significance of this decline, we should note that the population of Rome declined from a million citizens at its peak to less than 50,000 citizens at the end of its reign. Technology, in the broadest sense of the term, played an important role in the rise and fall of the Roman Empire and other social organizations that followed.

The Romans were able to build large structures, roads, and aqueduct systems that enabled their dominant position in society. The simple development of the arch played a significant role in the capacity of the Romans to build this infrastructure. While some people might characterize the development of such things as the arch as prescience, they played a role in the advancement of society the way science does today.

We have records of similar developments during the history of Cronin society. It is easy to assume that the development of science and technology follows some steady path to greater levels of sophistication. However, it is our conclusion that the development of science follows cycles which in turn has an impact on the social organization of intelligent life. There are three factors that have a major impact on the development of science and technology. One is the random factor which we have very little control over. One day by accident or intuition an individual develops a theory that something is following some natural order, which is then proved through experimentation. The second factor is the amount of resources data society devotes to the development of technology. The third factor is the number of skilled craftsmen or scientists to build the tools necessary to build infrastructure in general and more specifically the infrastructure of scientific investigation.

A good example of how this process works is the development of the Webb telescope. More than 30 years ago some scientists realized that they had to develop such a tool to understand the development of the universe hundreds of millions and billions of years ago. The project then required the funding of multibillion dollars required to build a telescope. Finally, it required the training and skills of thousands of people in various aspects of science and technology to build the satellite and launch it into orbit.

In an earlier period, the United States made the commitment to send man to the moon, land them on the moon, and then return them to earth. This was a huge undertaking, but the commitment was made to achieve this goal by the end of the decade in which the project was first launched. The primary reason for launching the probe toward Earth was to make sure that Earth did not present any kind of threat to Cronin society. But once the project was underway it was determined that the probe could also be used to gather valuable information regarding how cultures interact with technology and its impact on the environment. After a short time, we realized that the Earth was significantly out of balance with conditions that would allow for long-term viability of the human species. Despite this distressing information, we were still committed to our original goal of not contacting the society we were observing. However, when we discovered that Cronin society had a limited future, we, somewhat selfishly, decided that human society could provide a legacy for Cronin society. Thus, we made the decision to contact you.

The main issue that we see is because of the overuse of technology and Earth's resources, human society has created conditions that will lead to its ultimate demise. Nature that exists on Earth and the Cronin planet adjusts to changing conditions. While the Earth will continue for millions of years adjusting to changes in the balance of forces. The fossil record and the geological record reveal that the planet Earth has gone through some very radical changes in the past. These changes were so significant that for long periods of time, hundreds of millions of years, the Earth was not habitable by life in almost any form. There are many ways that this balance displays itself. When the earth was impacted by a large asteroid 66 million years ago conditions on earth changed immediately from a condition that allowed dinosaurs to live for almost 200 million years, as the dominant species on the planet.

On a smaller scale, scientists have determined the impact of removing a predator from the environment. Many would believe predators did not serve any useful function in the balance of nature. But studies have shown that it was the primary balancing factor in maintaining a stable environment. The predator preyed on certain species of animals for its existence. When the predator was removed, this species that it had preyed on multiplied unchecked and in turn consumed plant life to the extent that it could no longer support the larger number of pray animals. Using technology, the human species has exploited certain resources such as petroleum and other fossil fuels to produce carbon dioxide and other gases that contribute to global warming in amounts well more than the gases that would be produced if the human society was still just relying on muscle and animal power alone to provide the means for survival.

Scientific discovery does not progress in a straight line or even an exponential line like you have experienced since you started with this process. Scientific discovery goes through cycles where there is high activity and then relatively low activity. This seems to be due to discoveries of certain key technologies. For example, your recent very rapid advances in digital technology have resulted from first development of microcomputers and then the ubiquitous use of cell phones which have incorporated the technologies that used to be stand-alone like digital photography.

The rapid advance in technology is often driven by market forces where one company's competing with another continues to develop more and more features and functionalities just to get an advantage over its competitor rather than solving a specific problem or issue. This high development leads to market saturation which in turn reduces the incentive to develop additional technology.

On earth today technology is used as a tool to enhance the activities of humans which are the primary actors. As you develop artificial intelligence there is some fear that machines could take over. When we encountered this on Cronin, we quickly realized improving biological life was and still is the primary motivator. Biological beings have basic needs such as in taking energy as food, reproducing, and raising new generations. All species have engaged in these activities including humans over many millions of years. Just as your society has decided now to use genetic engineering to produce super individuals, we decided there was no need to develop technologies that would allow intelligent beings to become part of machines and leave behind their biological needs. I think our space probe is the best example of this.

In situations where biological beings could not undertake certain tasks, we develop sophisticated mechanical tools to enhance the activities and efforts of biological beings. We also gained a greater appreciation for the ability of nature to develop capabilities for biological entities and then transfer this information from generation to generation. The best example of this for humans is DNA, which provides not only the instructions to build new generations but also provides a history of the evolutionary process that occurred to arrive at the biologic entity that exists today. Finally, we have learned that there are many physical limits beyond which it is not possible to develop better technology. The best example of this is fusion technology which powers all the stars in the universe. Once we developed a controlled application of this technology there was no need to do any further research into other technologies.

We have learned that you use the expression a solution in search of a problem. In other words, some areas of technology reach the end point in terms of development and there's no need for any additional work in that area. We also developed an appreciation for the fact that not all aspects of existence are driven by technology.

Art, music, and other activities such as recreation enhance the quality of life. In fact, since there is some artificial aspect to technology in human terms some people strive to live a simpler life."

Neil then wrote the following e-mail to Gus. "I would like to share with you some of my reflections regarding our interaction and the impact that it will have on Earth's society. Galileo, who could be considered the father of astronomy, created a paradigm shift in the thinking of people during his time in the 17th century. He developed the telescope which he then used through observation to determine that the Earth was not the center of the universe but instead revolved around the sun. Furthermore, from making observations of our moon he determined that it had craters, valleys, and mountains which indicated that it was a celestial object like Earth rather than some disc attached to some kind of ring circling our planet.

His work was the beginning of science which also was the beginning of the controversy between religion and science. When his work was published, he was excommunicated from the Catholic Church which at the time was considered the authority on all things celestial. I wonder what Galileo's experience would be if he could have had access somehow to the information on our Internet today. At the very least, he would be looking 400 years into the future regarding the development of science and technology. Fast forward today to our encounter I am experiencing a similar look into the future which would be even a greater leap than 400 years.

I further reflected on the ability of humans to absorb information over a much shorter time frame than the time it took to develop the knowledge in the first place. On a day-to-day basis in life on earth today, older people who did not grow up with new technology, often asked their children who grew up with it how to use certain functions or capabilities of the system which younger people seemed to be absorbed by osmosis. If you extend this phenomenon to the overall process of learning it is very encouraging. Over some time. Humans developed the ability to communicate via speech. We do not know how long or how this process took place. But today a human infant is born without any ability to speak, but within a few short years it can communicate with others in the language it was born into. Over the last few 100 years our society has developed a wide range of technology such as electricity, television, computers, and cell phones. No one even considers specifically training infants in the use of electricity, television, and other applications of science to daily life. Even within the span of one generation we have experienced changes in the way we use technology without even noticing that the change is taking place.

For example, when television was first developed it was controlled via a set of switches and dials located on the television. As a matter of convenience remote controls were developed. Older people lose track of when this change took place and younger people assumed it was always that way. It could be said that technology is the great equalizer. Through the profit motive and mass production, capabilities can be made available to everyone even people with limited resources. In our society, this cell phone is the greatest example of this. I once saw a picture of a young boy in India driving a horse-drawn cart and talking on the cell phone. Because cell phones have become so affordable, they're essential to all commercial activity regardless of income level or economic development of the country in which people live. I have also seen pictures of refugees fleeing one country with only the clothes that they have on their back, but they do have a cell phone which is essential to their journey."

Chapter Six

The President was sitting in the Oval Office on one of the couches in front of the Resolute Desk. On the coach opposite him was Mike Rivers, his chief of staff.

"You know, Mike, this experience with the Cronin people brings me back to my high school years. I was the valedictorian of my class in a relatively small town. I was a big fish in a little pond. When I got to college, I was now among people many of whom, while not valedictorians, were near the top of their class. Then I was not that special anymore. We in the United States think we live in the greatest country in the world and know that our species dominates this planet. Now it's humbling to know that other planets are inhabited with intelligent life that has achieved an even higher level in their environment."

President John Adams had a rather unique background. He grew up with a father who believed in a very structured environment and discipline. As a result of living in this environment, John entered the seminary after completing his college work. After a couple of years, either fortunately or unfortunately as you would view it, John left the seminary basically because he was too much of an independent thinker to work well within the confines of the Catholic Church.

The President said, "Mike, you know we've been together for a long time, and I don't think we face a bigger challenge now than at any other time in the past. I am sure you heard about our opportunity to transfer technology from a society that's well-advanced past our current state of technological development.

I think it is fair to say that our contact with the Cronin society has reached biblical proportions. There isn't much difference between our communicating with the society that has had 3000 more years to learn about the world we live in and is located 35 light years away, than Moses going up onto the mountain to get 10 commandments from God, who was represented as the burning bush.

Furthermore, we have seen the traditional roles of science and religion reversed. We are relying upon our experience with the advancements we have been able to achieve with science to have the faith that those advancements will continue, and they will continue to be beneficial. It is easy to express our current dilemma with our enjoyment of guilty pleasures such as air travel, the use of gas-powered automobiles, and all the benefits we enjoy from electricity generated from carbon-producing fuels which will eventually result in us being punished with the flood produced by global warming and the melting glacial ice.

Relatively speaking, the level of sophistication of some parts of society today in science and its capabilities is not much different from the understanding of society thousands of years ago regarding religion. Religion has been society's way of dealing with a dangerous world. It helps us with the belief that we will be protected from this dangerous world by a power greater than ourselves.

I believe that a significant portion of our society today is willing to believe that the elections can be rigged in favor of the winning party although there is no evidence that such rigging occurred. People are willing to suspend disbelief to support a change in the social order that will protect them from or reverse the disadvantages they have experienced because of increased technology. Economists have told us that jobs lost in one sector of the economy will eventually be absorbed by other parts of the economy. However, I believe that there are limits to this process. The jobs that are eliminated because of increased technology allow workers to move into new jobs of greater levels of sophistication. But there is a logical end to this process. It is conceivable that there could be a society someday where technology has replaced all jobs where activities that we characterize as work have been eliminated.

"Yes, Mr. President, I've heard about it, and I agree there will be significant challenges especially from a political standpoint," replied Mike.

The president continued, "To paraphrase an old expression, all technology is not good for all the people all the time. Hydroelectric power generation is the most efficient way of generating electricity and its completely carbon-free. On the other hand, there are people who want to remove dams to restore the landscape to the way it was before the dam, although we have a significant need for carbon-free power sources. Then you have the people who we refer to as 'not in my backyard' who agree in principle with the advantages of certain technology but don't want it built close to them if it has some negative impact on them. Finally, you have companies like typewriter companies that are put out of business by new technologies such as microcomputers. The factory and the machinery needed to produce an electromechanical device are completely unaligned with the process of manufacturing circuit boards and other electronic components.

Our challenge is made even greater by our current polarized political situation. Our recent experience with the pandemic is a good example. While masks and vaccines are essential to combating something like COVID-19, some people can make them political footballs that inspire people to resist because they feel that their personal freedom is being impinged, regardless of the overall benefit to society.

I would like to get your thoughts on this today, and I'm sure we'll talk about it many times in the coming months."

"Mr. President, I would be glad to offer you my thoughts on how we could best address these challenges. As you know, I had a wide range of experience in business before I got into politics. I believe I have a perspective that might provide some solutions to the challenges we face.

As I see it, in its most basic sense, we are dealing with the transfer of intellectual property. On the one hand, we must recognize the rights granted to the owners of existing technology as they are protected under the patent system.

On the other hand, as you know, the federal government often engages in research and development in areas which are too risky for the private sector to undertake. The government then, in turn, turns technology over to the private sector for it to develop it. Ironically, I think we can find many examples in the space program, where NASA set the specifications and then cooperated with the private sector to build rockets and satellites that produced both military and civilian benefits.

I am sure that the biggest challenges will come with the implementation of new technologies and industries that will replace existing technologies and industries. Most likely the one industry that will be affected the most will be the fossil fuel industry. There is no question that companies in this sector are facing the challenge of switching out of fossil fuels to other noncarbon-producing fuels and sources of energy. However, I think they are in no way prepared for the rate of change that will occur if we implement fusion technology, which has already been successfully implemented somewhere else. Unfortunately for us, working with the fossil fuel industries will present significant challenges since it already has significant facilities in place to influence public policy regarding their industry. The challenges will range from leasing offshore resources to taxation, which supports road construction and other infrastructure in this country.

On a global basis, the petroleum industry has significant consequences. Since the time of the first oil embargo, we have witnessed the significant power that countries with significant oil resources have had on geopolitics. Many of these countries generate a significant portion of their gross national product from the export of oil.

I have only addressed one industry so far. I am sure that the pharmaceutical industry will be as affected or affected by technologies we may get from our alien friends.

In general, there will be a requirement for significant reeducation of existing professionals in the various scientific disciplines. Hopefully, they can make the transition and start from a place that is significantly advanced from where they are now. This will most likely require significant participation on the part of the academic community. There is a risk that this significant advance in the various disciplines will have a disincentive for innovation for a while until all the new knowledge can be fully processed. There's no sense in continuing to work on a product or process that has already been developed by our friends from another planet.

The task of implementing the technology and handling the transition required by it will require the establishment of a separate government agency that will oversee the distribution of the technology to whoever wants to make the investment necessary to develop products and services based on this technology.

Public utilities will be less affected by the introduction of fusion technology than the petroleum industry. The electric utilities already bill separately for distribution and allow customers to purchase energy from suppliers other than their primary utility. The petroleum industry is going to be strapped with a lot of infrastructure for exploration and refining that cannot be easily repositioned. The petroleum industry can count on the fact that there is a large installed base of gas-powered vehicles which will be slowly replaced by electric vehicles. Under the worst-case scenario, the total stock of gasoline-powered vehicles will not be completely replaced by electric vehicles for many years.

In addition, there are other uses for petroleum such as plastics, tires, etc. At least based upon what we know about aviation, petroleum will most likely still be the fuel in this sector. Since the public utilities are already regulated and can adapt by converting the heat-generating facilities and power plants from fossil fuels to fusion technology, all the equipment involved with electric generators, etc., should still be useful. I suggest, based on all that I've already mentioned, an approach of cooperation rather than forced implementation will work best.

During the period they must be phased out as a transportation fuel, petroleum companies should engage in an accelerated phase of diversification. The tobacco

119

companies did it in the '70s when they anticipated that there would be a significant decline in smoking because of the ban on advertising on television.

I think that a major part of the polarization in our society today is the result of significant numbers of people being made obsolete by new technology which has been further aggravated by outsourcing services and manufacturing to countries abroad. Till now most people have made the transition required by technological change on their own. Of course, there are some retraining services that are offered by state unemployment programs to help in the transition. But we're going to have to step this up a few notches with a federal program. We will have to find a way to fund this effort by taxing the early implementation of the new technology. A model for this may be how we tax petroleum sales to provide for infrastructure development and road maintenance. In fact, we may need a Commission to design the Commission.

Unfortunately, we live in an age where there is a distaste for big government; however, unusual circumstances justify unusual means. It's hard to say where we would have been during the depression if we didn't have all the programs that got things going and provided work for all the unemployed."

Chapter Seven

Thomas Miller, the editor of the Washington Observer, was meeting in his office with Henry Adams, who was the paper's chief science writer.

"Henry, there are rumors that we have been contacted by extraterrestrial intelligence. This would be just another outlandish rumor if it wasn't for the fact that there has been a lot of activity going on of a secret nature. If our sources are correct, this could be the scoop of the century. On the other hand, it could be our biggest blunder ever.

You may be aware of the broadcast in 1938 by Orson Welles; it was a fictitious reporting of a landing by extraterrestrial life that had overcome the military of the United States in short order. Although the radio broadcast was meant to be fictitious, and the broadcasters thought that no one would believe it was true, many people thought it was true and there was widespread chaos at the time. I just bring this up to give you a sense of how disruptive contact with extraterrestrial life would be. It could cause widespread concern even if the contact was not of an aggressive nature. Extraterrestrial life could provide us with advances in science and technology that would make many of our existing technologies obsolete. For example, if they had successfully used fusion technology, the low-cost energy from such an innovation would completely decimate some industries like coal and significantly reduce the revenue of the fossil fuel industry. I want you to make it your priority to find any sources that could confirm what we've learned so far."

"Well, Tom, that's extremely exciting, and you can bet I will enjoy following up on this one. In doing my reporting, I will be asking only what's going on with all this secret activity without mentioning anything about the possibility of extraterrestrial contact."

As he was getting up to leave the office, Henry started running down the list in his head of some of the people he would contact. At the same time, he was thinking how exciting it would be to write a story about such a once-in-a-lifetime experience.

With all the advances in technology and our own success in space travel since the War of the Worlds broadcast in 1938, the possibility of such extraterrestrial contact was a remote possibility that would be believable by a wide part of the population. The efforts by the SETI project and recent changes by the Defense Department regarding how they categorize unidentified flying objects just increase the believability of such extraterrestrial contact.

The first person that Henry would contact is Neil. Even if he had nothing to tell him about what's going on, he could provide a great deal of background information that could be used later if it got around to writing an article.

"Hi, Neil, this is Henry Adams at the Washington Observer. Do you have a few minutes to speak? I have always admired your ability to make space and related technology understandable to the average person. To get right to the point, we've heard a rumor that there has been some contact with extraterrestrial life. We know nothing about how it may be or how extensive it has been. In addition, we have been observing a lot of confidential activity that indicates that something must be up. My guess is that if it was just some radio contact from a planet many light years away, there wouldn't be any need to be confidential about it. It would be something that people would see in their morning news and say, 'Oh, that's nice, maybe in 100 years we'll meet them.' But if the contact could have implications in the next few years for humanity, then the reporting of this contact would have to be handled with extreme caution."

While Henry was speaking, Neil's mind was racing - already it's come to this, how do I handle this, he thought to himself. Neil was so excited about the original contact he didn't have time to think about how he would handle the situation he now was in. He couldn't lie as that surely would imply that he was a part of some kind of cover-up. Since the circle of people who already knew about the contact involved several people and was sure to be expanding rapidly as people did their jobs in pursuing the task they were given at the President's meeting.

Since Neil had worked with Henry on various projects in the past, he felt he had more than a passing understanding of his character and the ability to treat this information with the utmost discretion.

"Henry, I think you understand the extreme sensitivity of this matter. Seriously, anything I say is completely off the record. I will deny anything if anything comes back to me. I would much rather work with you as a responsible journalist who will know how to handle this situation as it develops rather than some hack who will be strictly after the sensationalistic nature of such a story.

I feel the best way that we can proceed with this is I will acknowledge that we have made some contact but will not give you any more details at least at the present. I would ask that in your reporting, you check back with me about what you have learned. I'm not saying that I would give you permission, that's up to you and I can't do that; on the other hand, I can verify the veracity of anything that you may learn. In other words, we're in this together to do our best to handle this in the matter that has the best long-term outcome for humanity.

The next logical organization to contact would be SETI, which has been the coordinating organization for the search for extraterrestrial intelligence.

"Hello, Rebecca, this is Henry Adams from the Washington Observer. I'd like to ask you a few questions today if I may. Are you about to report anything regarding finally contacting an extraterrestrial intelligence?"

"No, Henry, things here are as usual, lots of searching and waiting but nothing concrete to report at this point. Why do you ask? Have you heard anything that prompted your call to me today?"

"Well, Rebecca, I can't disclose my source, but there appears to be some indication that, in fact, that is the case. I wish I could tell you more, but I don't have very much more to tell you. Thanks for your time."

Henry thought to himself, well if he had good information that contact has been made but it did not come through the results of any of our searching activities. That could only mean that the contact was initiated by the extraterrestrial intelligent society. Henry thought further to himself, this sounds like the beginning of a good movie plot.

Henry was roommates with a guy at MIT who now has a pretty high-level position in the Department of Energy. Henry thought he'd give him a call and see what he could find out.

"Hello, Justin, this is Henry, your old roommate at MIT. How has life been treating you? Are you still playing rugby?"

"Well, Henry, it's good to hear from you after all these years. No, I had to give up rugby about a year or two ago because it was taking too much out of my body. I am now confined to running two or three miles every day to keep in shape. How about you?"

"Justin, it's pretty much the same here. I am enjoying my job working here at the paper; it gives me the chance to get exposed to new things all the time. I'm not stuck at a desk pursuing some two or three-year project which may not lead to anything in the long run.

Justin, I've got a favor to ask. There are rumors going around that we're near a breakthrough in fusion technology. Is there anything that you can share with me in this regard?"

"There is definitely something going on with regard to fusion technology, but I really can't tell you much more than that. People are asking a lot of questions that would indicate we have to be prepared for some developments in this area. We haven't been given very much background information with the requests. After working here for as long as I have, I know when not to ask questions where information would have been volunteered with the request.

"Tom, this is Henry, just wanted to give you an update on this fusion technology story. I have been able to determine there's something that is going on based on the level of disclosure from the people I was able to talk to. It must be something big. Over the years we have been making incremental progress in this area where none of the individual steps would result in life-changing developments in the short term. Based on what I've been able to learn so far, it looks like we're going to have to wait for some announcement in this area. Meanwhile, I will get up to date on all the recently disclosed information with regard diffusion technology to be prepared to best cover any announcements that are made.

Chapter Eight

Neil was just completing a meeting in his office when he got a text from his wife.

"Meet you at 6:30 at the Left Bank," a restaurant in the Columbus Circle area.

It was Neil's 32nd wedding anniversary.

The Left Bank was one of 1000s restaurants in Manhattan that served good food with prices to match. When COVID-19 struck, the restaurant had to close like many across the country during the pandemic. It survived, just about, by selling its $40 and $50 entrees as takeout food delivered by Uber. While the restaurant survived, many of its wait staff did not make out as well.

Working as a server at an upscale restaurant provided the opportunity to make a decent living provided you lived in Queens or the Bronx and commuted to work.

Neil's wife, a leading Broadway actress, was equally affected as Broadway shut down completely. COVID was one of those events that comes out of nowhere and affects everyone's lives rich and poor alike.

Unfortunately, the well-to-do managed to survive better than people in the lower levels of the economy. It was such a significant event that it even changed people's behaviors and attitudes regarding family versus work and working at home or in the office. The impact was so great that the term pre-COVID and post-COVID had meaning to everyone.

Neil wondered if the same terminology would be used to characterize time periods either pre-contact or post-contact.

Neil entered the restaurant, and his wife was already seated in the back. The restaurant was one of those long narrow affairs that were common in New York, built on the ground floor of brownstone buildings. His wife Tara raised her hand to get his attention, and he walked over to the table and sat down. Tara had already ordered a bottle of champagne, and it was sitting in an ice bucket by the side of their table.

Neil reached for the champagne and poured some in each of their glasses.

Tara made the toast. "Here's to 32 wonderful years and looking forward to another 30 wonderful years. My, have things changed since we first met."

"True," Neil replied, "but some things change faster than others. If someone from the 1850s came into your theater today, they would know what's going on and why. On the other hand, if someone from the 1850s came into the Space Center, they would be blown away. Both by the architecture and the fact that we were presenting information to the public that was not even known by astronomers at the time.

Now increase the time gap to 2500 years. A person coming into your theater wouldn't understand the electric lights but would understand what was going on and why. Again, compare this experience to the experience of someone from 2500 years ago entering the Space Center. That person from 2500 years ago would still be blown away by the architecture, by the materials such as glass and aluminum vinyl, and all the other materials that we use today in everyday construction. That person may not even know what the Space Center was about. Astronomy was still the business of philosophers rather than scientists."

"You know Neil, there may be a lot more to your observation than appears at first. When we think about contact with extraterrestrial intelligence, we think about advanced accomplishments in science such as physics in astronomy. But intelligent activity involves a lot of other things besides science. If you look back in history of civilization, you can go back to Roman times or the times of

Greece and see things like sculpture and architecture. Also, since the Greeks had amphitheaters, one must assume that some type of entertainment took place in these theaters. As you know from the writings of Aristotle and Socrates, much thought went into what the right form of government may be and other thinking regarding ethics.

One could speculate that is the reason there is less perceived change in what I do in the arts than you do in the sciences. Maybe this is because human progress regarding the arts had already made significant progress 2500 years ago while science was still a speculative philosophical activity.

If you fast forward to today, the arts take advantage of science to enhance the impact of the arts. If you look at the amount of time people spend regarding the arts such as music, movies, television, even sporting events, most people will agree that all of this activity increases the quality of life just as much as the improvements we gain from science in areas like medicine.

I know that your focus is on technology transfer, but there might be things to learn by comparing our social development with development that has taken place on Cronin. It could be possible that we have made more productive advancement in areas such as politics. It has been said that the United States has progressed economically and politically due to the forethought of our founding fathers.

It appears that there is consistency regarding physics throughout the universe because the laws of physics concern themselves with the behavior of physical matter and energy. On the other hand, the arts relate to life as it has developed and is being lived in a specific environment. Since life accommodates to its environment maybe politics and other aspects of non-science develop according to the needs of the environment rather than some universal laws."

"You're right," Neil replied, "it's an interesting question which suggests that social scientists should participate in the information exchange with the Cronin people. For example, if you think about where the science of psychology is today, it's at a completely different place than the explanations for human behavior that we were provided when religious organizations were also involved with government.

Next time that I contact Gus on Cronin, I will raise these issues with him. Thanks for sharing your thoughts on this with me. Always pays to get the benefit of a different perspective no matter what you're talking about."

"So how has your day been?" she asked.

"Well, we haven't fully digested the fact that we've been contacted."

While the whole affair was top secret it wasn't anything that Neil didn't share with his wife. They both talked in general terms so that any close by person who might be eavesdropping would know exactly what they're talking about. In New York, well-known personalities have a little more freedom from fans bothering them when they are spotted in public places like restaurants and department stores.

Neil continued, "it's like being in a dream and I'm going to wake up at any minute. I had a meeting in the president's office yesterday with a group of key people. This contact was totally unanticipated. Yes, we're playing this by ear to see how things go step by step.

How was your day?" Neil asked.

"Well, they're still looking for the last few investors for the play. It's always crazy process one day you're scrambling like crazy to find investors and the next day you've got three or four bidding to get in on the action. You could say that I'm in the same situation too. Although we've gone through this process many times before, it's like you're going through this for the first time. I'm really looking forward to it. We've got a great playwright, and they think the plot is very contemporary.

Chapter Nine

The vice president was 59 years old. He met his wife, Barbara, while attending Texas State University. Shortly after graduation, they got married, and in the next few years, they had two daughters. In the early years of their marriage, Barbara was content to be a stay-at-home mom while Bob started a career in marketing for a Fortune 500 corporation. Since he had a strong interest in politics, Bob started out as a part-time politician as the mayor of the small town they lived in. As would be the case with many a politician, he moved on and upward as time went by, making politics his full-time occupation.

Bob came from a middle-class family. His father ran a local plumbing supply business for most of his life. On the other hand, Barbara came from a family that had been in the oil business for a couple of generations. When Barbara and Bob got married, her family had higher aspirations for her, but she was content being in love with Bob and supporting him in his ambitions. In addition, when she married, her father established a trust fund that provided about the income annually that she could earn at a good-paying job. When the girls started to attend college, Barbara started doing some volunteer work just to keep herself busy.

As time went by, they started to grow apart. At first, they stayed together for the sake of the children, and then later, they decided to stay together since it would be better for Bob's political career. Since neither of them had developed any serious relationship with someone, divorce was never considered. As Bob moved up from being a congressman to a senator, being a politician's wife also had some appeal to Barbara.

The Vice President's car drove up to number One Observatory Circle, which is located at The US Naval Observatory. The US Naval Observatory provides a wide range of astronomical data to the US Department of Defense and provides the official standard of time for the entire US. The residence, often referred to as the National Observatory, is the official residence of the Vice President of the United States. It was originally built in 1893 for the Chief of Naval Operations; however, Congress transferred it into the official residence for the Vice President through a temporary order, but it's still the official temporary residence of the Vice President.

The Vice President has an office in the White House, so his home is primarily a residence as opposed to the White House where official business is conducted and is considered by many a symbol of the presidency of the United States. But it's also where the President lives.

As the car pulled into the driveway, Bob asked the driver, "Do you have any plans for the weekend?" He responded, "I might do a little fishing if the weather holds out. You have a good weekend, Mr. Vice President."

As Bob entered the kitchen, Barbara was making a drink for herself. They had help to do that, but Barbara likes to do small things herself. She felt more at home doing that, and it was more like how it used to be before they moved to Washington.

"You're home early tonight for a change," Barbara said.

"Yes," Bob said, "I guess everybody needs a break, no matter how busy they are."

As the head of the task force, Bob spent a lot of time at work. During normal times, Bob had the typical routine of a Vice President, which was not the 24/7, 365 for the President.

"I know I'm not supposed to ask," Barbara said, "but can you tell me anything about what's keeping you so busy lately? Is it some international crisis that I should be worried about?"

While he couldn't share all the details, Bob thought maybe he'd let Barbara know a little bit about what was going on to ease her mind.

"There has been a significant breakthrough in the generation of electricity using fusion technology. As you know, we have been working on this for decades, and it's finally here. The availability of unlimited energy at practically no cost is going to have significant consequences for the US and global economy. Our task force is working on how to best introduce this technology with the least amount of disruption."

Bob figured he didn't have to say anything about the fact that the technology had come from an extraterrestrial source, which would have far greater implications for social order in the US and globally.

"That's amazing," Barbara said, "couldn't have come at a better time; we really need a source of energy that doesn't contribute to the global warming problem."

Immediately, Barbara thought to herself, what does this mean for her father and his business, which could be drastically affected by such technology.

Ironically, to change the subject, Bob asked, "Is your father still planning to come and see us next week?"

"So far, everything looks good for that," Barbara said.

****

Everyone had just finished singing happy birthday to Barbara's dad and now had broken up into either one-on-one or small group conversations while they ate their red velvet birthday cake. Barbara was chatting with her dad.

"I'm so glad that I have been able to spend this day with you. I remember that you always made it to our birthday parties when we were kids no matter how busy you were."

"Yes," her dad replied, "those years go by quickly, and I didn't want to miss any one of your birthday parties."

"So, dad," Barbara said, "are you thinking of slowing down to enjoy yourself and maybe get to see us a little bit more often?" Barbara thought that it would be best to approach the issue with fusion energy as a retirement issue with her dad rather than getting into any issue of disclosing information she got from Bob.

"You know, I thought of it many times, but every time I think I'm still having a good time doing what I've always loved to do."

"Well, dad, I guess you gotta do what you gotta do, but there are a lot of changes coming for the oil industry, especially with the fast growth of electric vehicles. Only a year or two ago, you saw one on the road occasionally. Now, when I drive around town, I see at least two or three every day. Now's a good time to retire; things are probably not going to be much better than they are now, and you are entitled to retirement. When technology change gets going, it really goes fast. When cell phones first got started, only a few people who could afford the high monthly fees had phones, and they were bulky. Now, you know everyone older than 10 has one, and you can't separate people from their cell phones even for a few hours."

Barbara's uncle walked up and started to have a conversation with their dad. Meanwhile, Barbara saw her sister motioning her to come over.

Chapter Ten

The petroleum industry was holding its annual conference on safety and exploration in a major hotel in New Orleans. The emphasis of the conference was more on information exchange rather than a trade show with a lot of flashy booths. It was not the kind of conference that's covered by the mass media and even only by some of the industry-specific media.

The conference provided an opportunity for the key executives in the industry to get together and compare notes about almost anything that applied to the business. A meeting of 10 key executives was taking place in a private dining room in one of the upscale restaurants in town. While the executives were not doing anything that could be considered illegal, they didn't want to draw attention to the fact that they were meeting. In the past, topics had been about overall industry trends that affected everyone and explored mutual approaches to the challenges presented.

A hearty meal was enjoyed by all, featuring some of the best Cajun cuisine. Everyone was having coffee, and a few were smoking cigars. All the attendees were male. To focus the conversation, one of the executives asked if he could have everyone's attention.

"Gentlemen, I have learned that there is the potential for a breakthrough in fusion technology. Just to remind you, this technology offers significant energy output without any of the negative aspects of spent fuel rods and reactor meltdown. Based on what we've been able to learn about what's going on in Washington, it appears that this breakthrough might be much more substantial than the crazy scenario we went through in 1978 when two professors from the University of Utah announced that they had discovered a way to produce fusion at room temperatures. You may remember at the time it was called cold fusion.

Scientists have been working on fusion technology for decades and still seem to be a decade away from a practical application of this technology. In other words, it is only a small consideration in our planning for future development and marketing programs. On the other hand, I know that your companies all have programs to plan for the ultimate transmission away from petroleum products in energy generation and transportation. If this breakthrough is true, we might have to make significant changes in the timeline for this adjustment.

I would like to have your thoughts on how we can face this existential threat to our industry. I would like to know if you believe we should face this issue with the united front. Or should each company do its best to adjust to the requirements of changing infrastructure, marketing programs, and public awareness."

George from Texkan Oil spoke first.

"John, I'm glad that you brought up the topic. In recent years, we have had a mixed track record handling

149

research regarding global warming. While we might have been able to hold off the transition from fossil fuels, in the long run, we may have created existential problems that are beyond our capacity to address.

I know that we all thought we were doing the right thing at the time, but we do not have much ability to hold off the inevitable. Fusion technology is a matter of physics, and there is no denying it will eventually work. Furthermore, there are fewer counterarguments that can be made for this technology such as problems with disposal of spent fuel rods, etc., which are involved with fission technology.

We live in an age where technology has become almost like religion for a good segment of the population. This ignorance can be exploited, but only for a certain period, then we all must face the music. I will have to get approval from our board, of course, but I am willing to commit the resources of our company to best addressing this challenge."

Greg, an executive with more experience in the industry than anyone else in the room and only one generation removed from wildcatters spoke next.

"I believe we can't go off half-cocked on this issue. We have faced challenges in the past such as the oil embargo, and somehow, we got around them and conducted business as usual. If what you say is true, we could face a partial or complete liquidation of our industry as we know it today. I suggest that we explore ways that we can frustrate the implementation of this new technology if it really exists. Even with its problems, fission technology could have had wider implementation and benefits to the environment if it wasn't for the bad rap that it has had to live with in recent years, after such things as Chernobyl and Three Mile Island.

While we may not be able to hold it off forever, we should explore areas where we might be able to slow it down. In other words, we should not take this lying down or even offer to cooperate with the implementation. We all have stockholders, and it's just an ugly truth that stockholders in general are looking for the best bottom line possible despite the possible negative consequences."

Bill, the president of Coloco Oil, spoke next.

"We've been facing this issue for somewhere between 20 and 30 years. Back in the 80s and 90s, we had the best research facilities available to us, and we knew that we would eventually face a decline in demand for our product. Back then, we had an opportunity to take a proactive approach to the problem, but we chose to do otherwise. We were like people facing a storm, and rather than getting out of the way, we thought we could somehow change the course of the storm.

I think the core of this issue is the fact that we were looking at something that was not going to be a day-to-day issue for 20 or 30 years. Even executives in their mid-career knew that they could retire 20 or 30 years in the future without having a significant impact on their life. In other words, we said let's leave it up to the next guy.

Now we must find a way to get out of the path of the storm. We still have an opportunity to take a profitable approach to the problem. In the most basic terms, we are in the business of applying resources to a task that produces an economic return. I'm willing to pledge the resources of our company to this solution to whatever extent is required."

Finally, Jim, who was from the largest company in the industry, said,

"We're not dead yet. We have about 20 years left to transition out of motor fuels. We have some good data points, and if we combine those with our experience with the average life of a car, this means that we have until 2043 until we sell our last gallon of gasoline to cars and small trucks. There will be some market for gasoline sales for antique car owners and other small gasoline-powered engines such as lawn mowers, which will continue to produce some demand for gasoline. The key statistics that we have are:

- In 2022, it was estimated that there were 285 million cars and small trucks on the road.

- In 2022, approximately 13.75 million vehicles were sold in the US.
- In 2023, approximately 2 1/2 million electric vehicles were sold in the US. Nineteen states have already introduced legislation that will prohibit the sale of gasoline-powered new cars after 2034. There's a good chance that this will become a national requirement by that time. Thus, we are going to see a gradual increase in the number of electric vehicles sold in the US each year until it takes over the entire market of 13.75 vehicles sold in the US.

The 2023 car sales number was already down from 2017 when car sales exceeded 17 million vehicles. If we assume that electric vehicle sales will increase at the expense of gasoline-powered vehicles over 11 years, they will grow to 100% of the market. Adding up the cumulative sales of electric vehicles as they grow from two and a half million vehicles in 2023, there will be 96 million electric vehicles on the road in 2034.

If we further assume that every electric vehicle sale replaces a gasoline-powered vehicle, a key assumption in these calculations is that the primary time customers decide what type of vehicle they're going to purchase is when they're replacing their existing vehicle, which they are trading in or is no longer serviceable. From 2034 forward, every remaining gas-powered car will be replaced by an electric vehicle. Thus, it will take about 12 years to replace all the existing gas-powered vehicles on the road with electric vehicles.

Some people may say these numbers are still alarming. However, many other markets have gone through a transition from one form of technology to another. In the telephone industry, cell phones have completely replaced wireline phones for consumer communication over about the same time. All markets have their ups and downs and have a life cycle. Due to its large installed base of gasoline-powered vehicles, the petroleum industry has a much better ability to project its future and adjust accordingly.

Chapter Eleven

The Secretary of Energy had already arrived at the meeting with two people from his office; he arrived 15 minutes early. He believed that being on time, as one business executive said, is arriving 15 minutes before his scheduled time for the meeting. The director of fusion technology, Bob Jones, was entering the room with two of his managers. Only the Secretary of Energy knew the true purpose of this meeting, and Bob Jones wondered why there was such an interest in fusion technology at such a high level as the Secretary of Energy.

"Mr. Jones," began the Secretary, "it's a pleasure to receive your update on fusion technology and answer some of the questions you sent along with your request. I would like to provide a little overview before delving into specifics. As you most likely know, there are two types of nuclear energy: fusion energy and energy from a fission reaction. Fission technology was developed during the end of the Second World War and was used in the two bombs that were dropped on Japan to end the war. Shortly thereafter, fusion technology was developed. While both technologies were developed for military purposes and used as such, fusion technology has not progressed as well as expected for non-military applications.

Fission technology exploits the energy produced when an atom of radioactive material, such as uranium, splits into two atoms of other elements. This fission process releases heat and an electron that, when it interacts with another uranium atom, triggers another fission reaction. This is called a chain reaction. If sufficient fissionable material is placed together, it will start a chain reaction, resulting in an atom bomb for military purposes and in a nuclear power plant when the fission process is controlled by limiting the number of electrons that interact with other fissionable material.

Fusion takes place when two molecules of a special form of hydrogen are pressed together under great heat and pressure to form an atom of helium and give off significant amounts of energy. In military applications, an atom bomb is used to create the high temperature and pressure conditions inside a hydrogen bomb required to start the fusion reaction, which continues until all the fusible material is used up. The process happens very quickly, thus releasing a huge amount of energy in a very short period, creating an explosion known as a mushroom cloud. This is the same process that takes place in all stars, including our sun. The huge mass of the sun creates pressure and temperatures through gravity to start the reaction.

We have been trying to harness the fusion reaction for electricity generation for several decades. Several different types of technology have been developed and tested to create these extreme conditions of temperature and pressure. Creating thousands of degrees of heat required to ignite a fusion reaction and then controlling the reaction is not easy to do. Recently, there has been a significant breakthrough in this technology where more energy is released from the reaction than is required to start it. However, creating this reaction under controlled circumstances for practical electricity generation is still at least 10 years in the future.

You may have heard the term cold fusion. A cold fusion reaction takes place at room temperature by harnessing the energy as hydrogen interacts with certain metals, such as Palladium. In 1989, two chemistry professors at the University of Utah thought they had figured out how to harness this energy to create cold fusion. After a short period of excitement, it was not possible to conclude that the energy being produced by their apparatus was coming from nuclear fusion. On the other hand, some energy was being produced which could not be explained by our knowledge of chemistry at the time. If cold fusion is ever developed, it will be even more significant than the developments in fusion technology developed using high temperature and pressure.

In the decades since fission technology was first developed, engineering improvements have allowed this technology to be scaled down from generating facilities that are large enough to power a small city to facilities that can power an aircraft carrier and even down to a submarine. Radioisotope power sources have been an important source of energy in space since 1961. Nuclear fission reactors for space have been used mainly by Russia, but now new and more powerful designs are under development in both the USA and Russia. Plutonium-238 is the vital power source for deep space missions.

With the exceptions mentioned above, fission technology has mostly been implemented in large-scale facilities very similar to those powered by oil, gas, and coal. A key factor in this process is the fact that the energy generated must be used as soon as it is made. In some cases, it has been possible to get around this limiting factor by using energy produced during off periods to pump water into reservoirs, which is then released during periods of high demand to generate electricity through a hydropower facility.

Another limiting factor for large-scale fission reactors is the fact that the energy generated in a centralized location must be distributed through a system of poles, towers, and wires to get it from the place where the energy is generated to where it is used. In current fossil fuel generating facilities, the cost of distribution is often as great as or greater than the cost of producing energy in the first place.

The greatest promise of cold fusion is the potential to scale it down so that it could be used to power an individual automobile. The size of the reactor used to produce the energy that was thought to be fusion energy 30 years ago was no larger than a typical car battery. In many ways, it involved chemical reactions that are very similar to the reactions that take place today in a typical car battery. Even though it may never be possible to scale it down to the level of an individual automobile, there is a much higher probability that generators could be designed that could be used in a single residential home or even a small manufacturing facility.

Both fission and fusion technologies generate electricity without releasing carbon dioxide into the atmosphere, which is the primary cause of global warming. Nuclear fission reactors would be the cheapest way to produce electricity. But issues of uncontrolled reactions causing reactor meltdowns and the disposal of the fuel rods from reactors have limit to use of this technology. It takes centuries if not thousands of years for fuel rods to degrade to the point where they are no longer harmful to humans. Nuclear fusion reactors, when they are developed, will not produce any harmful by-products and can be controlled more easily to avoid meltdowns.

Nuclear reactors, especially fusion reactors, have been touted as a source of almost unlimited energy at practically no cost, in addition to their low carbon footprint. While fusion reactors will be very competitive with traditional generating facilities that use fossil fuels, there will be some costs.

While fission reactors have yet to be built and the cost of operating them has yet to be calculated, it is possible to speculate what the cost for both hot fusion and cold fusion power would be. One of the expected benefits of fission reactors will be that the cost of the fuel used will be very low compared to oil, gas, or coal. However, from an operating standpoint, hydroelectric facilities have a zero direct cost for fuel. Hydroelectric facilities tap into the normal cycle of evaporation from the sea and lakes, which condenses in rain and then flows down from higher altitudes to lower altitudes where the hydroelectric facility can capture the energy from gravity as the water flows through the generating facility. If the capital cost of building a dam is not considered and only the operating cost of operating a hydroelectric facility, where its fuel is virtually free, the operating cost of the facility for labor and maintenance translates to less than two cents per kWh. This less than 20% of the cost of generating electricity with hydrocarbons. Thus, fusion technology will enable low-cost energy, but it will not be free, as some people project.

Regarding cold fusion, if it is ever developed, it will be as low cost if not lower cost than the total cost of high temperature fusion generating facilities. If cold fusion is implemented on a scale comparable to the batteries currently used in electric vehicles today, this would allow owners of cars powered by cold fusion to avoid the electric distribution costs that they would incur if they powered their vehicle from the grid.

Currently, batteries for electric vehicles cost from $2000 to $8000 per vehicle and are designed to last for 100,000 to 150,000 miles of vehicle operation. Thus, electric vehicles would be able to travel many months without refueling and at a cost, using the high-end numbers of about $0.02 per mile.

Chapter Twelve

"Good afternoon, John," the president said as the Secretary of State walked into his office. "Good to see you. It's a great day, isn't it? I love these days in late fall when you can get your last bit of sunshine before it gets nasty."

The President's chief of staff was also seated on the couch. "Good to see you, John." "Good to see you too, Mike." As John was taking a seat, he said, "Mr. President, I really don't have that much to report to you. Much less than I expected when I first started getting this information together. For one thing, since there's no physical contact between anyone on Earth and Cronin, we're not going to worry about issuing visas or setting up an embassy," and he laughed a little. The President replied, "I guess most people won't be able to afford the airfare". We still must figure out what we must do. It will be much less than what we must do when we start establishing colonies on the moon. I guess we'll follow some of the same procedures we use in Antarctica.

On a serious note, my primary job is to deal with relationships between the United States and other sovereign states; this will not be an issue in this case. Especially since we know Cronin is facing its imminent demise. On the other hand, we will play some prominent role in whatever protocols are established in the future. We already host the United Nations in New York City. We expect that relationships between various sovereign states and the United States and among themselves will not change very much from how they were before our contact.

As you know, our primary role is to promote democracy and force stability around the world. We help to make the world a safer place and we help other nations in times of need and crisis. Unfortunately, the bad actors will continue to behave the way they have in the past. They will not expect our contact with Cronin to result in any restraints that don't exist. None of these roles will change very much because of contact. One area where we will play a major role is in negotiating any treaties that are required regarding sharing the technology transfer from the Cronin people. We will either do this directly or in coordination with the United Nations. Fortunately, we should not expect any major monetary expenditures to achieve these goals. The one area where we may anticipate some issues is the changing dynamics with the oil-producing countries. Rapid implementation of fusion technology will accelerate the transition away from oil as a source of energy. Fortunately, this process is already in place or is being anticipated. Many of these countries have enjoyed significant revenues from their natural resources and hopefully they are planning for alternative sources of revenue.

Hopefully our contact with Cronin will give the leaders of other countries a different perspective on the role of sovereign nations. Now leaders of other countries will see themselves as somehow related as citizens of planet Earth. Because they know there's more intelligent life than on our planet. As I am sure your other advisors have told you we're on uncharted ground. The best we can do is be vigilant and as transparent as possible as this process takes place.

As a personal observation, most science fiction we have seen is much more alarming than what has transpired in our current situation. All the movies, books, etc., portrayed the contact in terms of some hostile takeover of the planet, If you look at the reality that we have experienced it's really what we should have expected. A civilization that has the technology to contact us most likely has all the resources that it needs and would not have to come to this planet for those resources. One of the things that we now know, which we've only known in the last 100 years is that the universe is so vast any travel by an alien civilization to get these resources would be more than offset by the time and energy required to reach our planet."

Chapter Thirteen

"My fellow Americans, I want to talk to you tonight about a significant event. It is an event that we all thought about from time to time but never anticipated that it would occur in our own lifetime. We have been contacted by extraterrestrial intelligent life. First, I must say, no one needs to panic. The emphasis is on the word 'contact'. The intelligent society that has contacted us is 35 light-years away; that is a very long distance. Even if they could travel at the speed of light, which would be a significant accomplishment even for an advanced society, they would take 35 years to get here. Most importantly, the society that contacted us has no reason to come to Earth; they have all the resources they need to live their lives. In other words, there aren't going to be any green men running around in the fields of New Jersey as was portrayed in Orson Welles' famous broadcast "War of the Worlds."

They learned about our presence because of radio and television signals that started emanating from our planet when these communication technologies first developed. Our contact is taking place through a probe which this society sent to our moon about a decade ago. We believe that this society has nothing but the best intentions for Earth. While the primary purpose of launching the probe toward Earth was initially to determine if we were hostile and, more importantly, because of curiosity, which seems to be present in all intelligent life. Just as we have launched probes within our solar system, they are conducting similar investigations on an interstellar scale.

As a result of popular fiction regarding contact by extraterrestrial life, it is reasonable to expect that the contact was made by means of some general signal broadcast at our planet with the hope that someone on our planet would detect this signal and eventually respond. However, in this case, it was very specific, all the way down to a specific individual. This may appear unbelievable to many, but we will provide more details about this contact, which will allow you to believe it.

While the society that contacted us made a specific contact in the United States, we view our role mostly in a custodial role, which will eventually allow the benefits of the information received from this society to be shared worldwide. The long-term impact of our interaction with this new society will be beneficial to Earth. They can provide us with new technologies that will have a significant impact on our way of doing business, international relations, and contending with environmental issues such as global warming.

It is our intention to set up programs to minimize the impact of these new technologies on your daily life. We also intend to share this technology with the people of the world, which we hope will lead to a new era in international relationships.

We are in uncharted territory when it comes to contact with another extraterrestrial intelligence. There has been some scientific speculation as to how this might be handled, but most of the scenarios that were used were general, since we had no way of understanding what this intelligent society's intentions would be with regard to people on our planet.

Fortunately, in recent years, we have had some experience dealing with global issues such as nuclear nonproliferation, global warming, and dealing with the COVID-19 pandemic. This experience, while not perfect, makes me hopeful that we can make the best of this situation. We as a country, regardless of politics, have been able to accomplish great things that span administrations and even generations. The design and construction of the Interstate highway system and the continued maintenance of that system is one example. NASA, which is responsible for our own space exploration programs, is another good example.

We intend to protect current technology owners and businesses and industries that may no longer be as competitive, with a program that assists them during the transition. I know that many of you do not like big government, especially if it imposes itself on your daily lives. Therefore, I and the current administration will make every effort to minimize regulation and incorporate the private sector in any programs that result from the implementation of new technology.

We have not yet established a name for this program, but once it is established, I expect it to be on a cabinet-level position with the title of Secretary of External Technology Implementation. Someone once said, 'may you live in interesting times.' We are already living in interesting times. I am looking forward to the challenges we will face in the weeks, months, and years ahead. I am taking a very positive approach to these developments and ask you, my fellow Americans, to take the same approach. God bless America and goodnight".

Shortly after the president's address, Neil sent a quick email to the president congratulating him on his speech. He also informed him that he would be emailing a transcript of the speech, just in case our friends from Cronin did not receive it by monitoring the news broadcasts that carried the speech

Chapter Fourteen

As would be expected, the reaction of various leaders around the globe was mixed, but on balance, it appeared to be positive.

The Pope released a statement that said he felt that the contact with extraterrestrial life would not have any impact on the areas of faith and religious teachings. The statement also said that the church looks forward to positive outcomes from this contact in the areas of control of global warming and more equitable allocation of income between the developed world and the developing world.

The Secretary-General of the United Nations also released a statement that had a very positive view regarding these developments. The fact that humanity as a whole was contacted will encourage global thinking and global outcomes rather than national priorities, nationalism, and economic competition between developed countries such as the United States and China. The UN stands ready to provide the resources of its organization to implement any technology that will benefit the developing world. Furthermore, it is prepared to act as the arbitrator between developed countries regarding the benefits of implementing new technologies.

The head of the Organization of Petroleum Exporting Countries (OPEC) released a statement that indicated a sense of resignation. The OPEC countries have already been facing for years the ultimate decline in the use of fossil fuels for transportation and energy production. Any new technology that we get from celestial benefactors will most likely accelerate the trend. However, the negative consequences of global warming will affect everyone, even the countries in its organization. The OPEC countries have significant resources generated from their oil exports; these countries look forward to investing these resources in the implementation of new technologies, especially in countries of the developing world.

The president of Harvard University said that Universities are the primary source for new technology development as well as the training of future decision-makers in private industry and government. Universities will face a period of uncertainty as the existing branches of science such as physics, chemistry, astrophysics, and to a lesser extent biology, learn what new information will be gained from our extraterrestrial benefactors.

The President of the US Patent Office released a statement that it will be challenged regarding maintaining intellectual property rights of existing patent holders. New technology has always been an ongoing process where the Patent Office must determine which new technology claims are unique. Thus, it is already prepared to decide which technologies came from our new extraterrestrial neighbors is already covered by US patents. It anticipates it will have to use its review process to establish a new class of technologies that came from extraterrestrial sources and thus cannot be patented by others making a claim that they developed the technology. As with all patent applications there is full disclosure. Therefore, it is possible that society can start utilizing the benefits of this new technology. The office already does not allow people to patent the basic laws of nature. The new technology that comes from Cronin will fit into this category.

The US Treasury Department issued a statement that it would review taxes and fees that are used to maintain the Interstate Highway system and other transportation resources. Some taxing system on electric vehicles would have to be developed to replace the lost revenues that will result from declining fuel sales. It will offer an outreach program to state and local governments which also levy sales taxes on petroleum products.

The speaker of the House of Representatives and the Majority Leader of the Senate issued a joint statement that they hoped political leaders can put their differences aside regarding implementation of new technology which is to the benefit of all citizens both current and future generations. The release stated that obviously we are currently contending with the issues of global warming. Thus, they are optimistic that we have done a lot of the groundwork which will lead to a rapid implementation of new laws, etc. regarding technology and global warming.

Despite the comments by the leaders of the two houses of Congress, there were some radical politicians who presented significant objections. Some characterized the announcement as just a hoax to gain political advantage over the other party. It was just political grandstanding aimed at preventing any progress without the ability to present any meaningful alternative.

In general, one could say that all these statements revealed a great sense of uncertainty how all of these things would be accomplished. It appears that if anyone is going to take an opposing position to any one of the positive statements listed above, they haven't yet figured out what their arguments would be to take such contrary positions.

Chapter Fifteen

Neil was getting ready to head out of his office for home when he received a call from the president.

"Neil, have we heard anything new from our friends from Cronin? It's been seven days since we had any contact."

"It's true," Neil responded. "I haven't heard anything since I sent the transcript of your speech out seven days ago."

"Neil, you know I was concerned at the start that this would be some kind of hoax perpetrated to embarrass us. Trying to make us look like a bunch of people who believe in UFO sightings. I know that we seem to take all the precautions to verify the veracity of the contact. On the other hand, if you consider the capabilities of some of our major adversaries such as China or Russia, they may have even gone to the extent of placing a decoy on the moon so that it would provide proof that the communication was legitimate."

"How are the people over at SETI doing, locating a signal in the vicinity of where we think Cronin is located?"

"Mr. President, the fact that we have not been able to find any electronic transmission from Cronin does not mean they do not exist. As you may remember, one of the primary reasons they sent a probe in our direction in the first place was concern that we might have some malicious intent towards themselves. Part of their defense program might include a system of shielding their communication from leaking out of their planet. Furthermore, they may be using some communication system that operates at a frequency or data rate that we could not identify as coming from an intelligent source rather than just being part of the background noise that exists throughout the universe."

"I will send a quick message out indicating our concern."

"Thank you, Neil, have a great night."

After the president hung up, Neil thought about how we have become accustomed to instant communications. In the world of exploration 500 years ago, explorers set out on voyages that could last months if not years before anyone knew if they were successful and what new knowledge, they might bring back with them.

Chapter Sixteen

Neil thought that he would check his email for important messages before retiring. As he was scanning the emails, he noticed one from Gus. "Finally, after 29 days we have contact," he exclaimed. He read the following:

"Hi Neil, I'm sorry for the delay in getting back to you; it was not intentional. The system of communications that we have been using with dark energy seems to have some drawbacks which we do not understand. In the past, we have experienced a gap of several days when the communication system is not available. In any case, we have reconnected, and I would like to tell you a few things.

First, I would like to tell you a little about our planet. Our planet is about 140% the size of your planet, and about 40% is covered by water. Our day is about 33 hours long, and it takes our planet 465 days to make one revolution around our star. We have very little seasonal variation in the weather since our planet's axis is parallel to the axis of our star. Our current population is about one billion people. We evolved over time very much like you did on Earth. Based on what we have observed about life on Earth, it could be said that there must be some basic laws of nature which are much deeper than the basic laws of physics that we know as universal.

As I told you earlier, our primary reason for traveling 35 light years to your planet was to determine if your society could in any way present a threat to Cronin's existence. As time went by with the project, we realized that it would also be an opportunity to do some studying which could best be characterized as astro-anthropology.

While we have evolved to a higher level of technology than your planet, that evolution has taken a very short period relative to the development of human society or Cronin society. While the evolution of technology often gets significant attention, social behavior also involves evolution.

We believed that you might have something to learn from the history of your planet, and the information exchange would not be completely one way.

We have, in fact, learned that your social evolution was much different from the way social behavior evolved on Cronin. We have learned from researching your Internet that you have your own anthropology programs that study the interaction of more advanced societies with less developed societies, at least in terms of technology.

While our interaction has been primarily focused on our technology, we believe that there are other areas where we may provide you with our learnings that will benefit your society as much as our technology. Before I get into the details, I would like to point out some differences between what we both call science and bias.

Earth society has lived in an age of science for about 400 years. The essential part of science is the scientific method. The scientific method involves using data or observations gathered in accordance with specific procedures. These observations tell us that reality is or, in some cases, cause and effect. We observe what we believe is cause and effect and then we design a study or data gathering to either prove or disprove what intuition tells us is really fact. We design the experiment so that we gather information about all the things that we believe are causes, and then observe what effects the perceived causes have on the end results. On the other hand, bias is conclusions that we make based on intuition that may involve other factors that we may not even be aware of.

Not all things can be determined by the scientific method. The scientific method works well with physical things like what happens when wood burns. On the other hand, some things will most likely always be subject to bias such as the existence of God, however we may define God, because we cannot design an experiment that would prove the existence of God. The best that any scientist may say in this regard is that the universe appears to be orderly and that flows from intelligent design which is God.

Since the beginning of the age of science, the explanation of many things has moved from bias to science. Since the beginning of science, we have been able to use science to create technologies such as electricity, computers, fertilizer, and millions of other things that have made our lives longer and more comfortable. We are having a greater impact on the environment in which we live, and that change is occurring exponentially. Only a short time ago our impact on the environment was limited by the muscle powers of humans and service animals. Today we have energy from fossil fuels, nuclear energy, solar energy to mention just a few.

Scientific knowledge is expanding so rapidly that the ability of any one individual to understand and use this technology is impossible. The development of the Internet has greatly expanded our access to this knowledge, and the specialization of companies and people regarding different parts of the knowledge base has enabled the exponential expansion of the number of products and services available to the average person. It has been said that the average person today has access to products and services that were not available to a king 100 years ago. Today it takes 16 to 20 years of education to be an effective contributor to society.

Unfortunately, while the average citizen has a greater understanding of technology and what it can do for them, they have less of an ability to understand the basics of the scientific method and many of the biases that we acquire as we grow to become a part of society. In fact, recent studies have shown just living in today's environment causes us to have biases that we were not even aware of.

A good example of how bias can wrongfully influence society is the current experience with firearms. People acquire firearms because they feel that in these uncertain times, firearms will provide them with a greater level of safety. In fact, the opposite has resulted. Studies have shown that households with firearms suffer more negative impacts from firearms than households that do not have firearms.

Societies go through an interesting transition regarding science and bias. When there is no science regarding a topic, people rely on some explanation regarding reality. Before science, that was religion. Religion grants itself authority to offer an explanation it has given is true. Mostly the authority given by religion is revelation passed down from others and accepted by those people based upon faith and the person making the revelation. The authority given to that revelation is often cloaked in mystery. The religious truth often originates in myths which are passed from generation to generation via verbal communication.

The authority of science comes from consistent repeatable results today that are the same as the results that were observed at some time before. This consistency is provided by written results recorded over time. Data recorded in books that were written. The process of recording and storing the books is a continuation of a process carried on by religious organizations regarding dogma. This process, when it is done regarding science, is called the scientific method. The process performed by scientists when the process first started was based on books which recorded the data and the laws that were derived from the data.

Today all information is stored on the Internet. Unfortunately, there is no control organization that controls or, more importantly, authenticates what is stored on the Internet. In fact, since the Internet is now used to sell products and services, the information is displayed with the bias requested by people with things to sell.

When people rely on the information they get from the Internet search, they are not aware of the biases. In any case, these biases have an impact on social behavior.

One could characterize the social development on Earth, at least during the period of recorded history on Earth, as leading to a behavior where one society with greater technological development, which I characterize in the broadest terms such as the means of warfare, dominates another society with lesser developed technology.

An example of this interaction is what happened when the European culture interacted with indigenous people in the Americas. Societies that existed in the Americas for tens of thousands of years and evolved with their own social values eventually were dominated and, in some cases, eliminated via contact with technologically advanced societies.

An experience in North America regarding the misapplication of technology couldn't have a better example than what happened with the Buffalo. The Buffalo had roamed the plains for 100,000 years and were in complete balance with the environment. When the Europeans came in with new technology such as steam-driven trains and rifles, the Europeans were able to almost eliminate the Buffalo. The last few years of this interaction are the most telling. Hunters by the thousands went out and slaughtered Buffalo just for their hides. Near the end, hunters had one great year and produced a great number of hides with the expectation that the same would be the case in the following year. They had no way of knowing how many Buffalo there were and what part of that population they were eliminating by their activities. It turned out that after their best year the following year there were no Buffalo left to be shot and skinned. That year the hunters were stunned that there was no longer any Buffalo for them to hunt.

On a global basis, the process which you call colonization was also a way that more developed societies exploited less developed societies. While the United States managed to free itself from the colonization established by European countries through a revolutionary war, other countries continued to be colonies of European countries until the early 1900s.

The most significant aspect of this exploitation process was not evident to those who did the exploitation. I guess it takes the evaluation of someone like us to realize how significant that behavior was. This process still exists today in different ways on Earth. The most basic aspect of this exploitation process is that it's built into the social fabric of the exploiters, and they believe that it is the natural order of things to engage in such behavior. Not only is it acceptable, but it is rewarded in terms of wealth and ways of living.

Let me give you an example that may help you understand how this bias works. When European settlers came to the United States, they viewed the indigenous people as savages that were not equal in status to themselves. Furthermore, they had very little value for their system of social behavior. In fact, this difference in behavior allowed European settlers to exploit indigenous people.

The indigenous people who occupied the land that is now called the United States had been there for thousands of years and developed a much more communal set of social values. For example, indigenous people did not believe that any individual could own land; rather, land was provided by a creator to be used by everyone for the communal benefit. This concept extended to natural resources such as buffalo herds which provided for most of what was needed to live. Europeans, on the other hand, going all the way back to Greek and Roman times, believed that people's status and their right to various resources was a right of birth. The ethics of the time taught that certain people were granted higher levels in society by a creator simply by the accident of their birth.

This ethic is the predominant ethic in a major portion of Earth society especially in terms of technology. People who develop technology are entitled to the rewards this technology enables. This process transfers part of the wealth of society as a whole from certain people to other people. This ethic is still very evident today in your business organizations where a few people at the very top are entitled to exceptional benefits simply because of their position as opposed to the rank-and-file people in their organization who are the actual source of these benefits.

I have mentioned these things as an introduction to my warnings with regard to the use of artificial intelligence. I can't resist seeing what two intelligent societies think about artificial intelligence.

Of all the technology that we can provide to Earth, artificial intelligence is probably the most valuable. Your society is just now starting to understand the capabilities and implications of the development of artificial intelligence. Until today, technology has, in one way or another, been a way of replacing human activity, either physical or mental, with technology. For example, tractors and fertilizers allowed 90% of the population that once lived on farms to move into cities and be employed in other activities. This migration was further impacted by the industrial revolution that mechanized many of the processes done by trades for centuries. In recent years, human activity has been replaced in the intellectual area by software programs that allow the quicker and more efficient gathering of data and the analysis of that data or ways of presenting information to management.

Artificial intelligence has the potential to replace many of the people who currently engage in the scientific process to produce new technology. While there are many social implications to artificial intelligence one of which is the potential nightmare that the machines take over, I would like to discuss with you one of the possibilities that may occur if we transfer our artificial intelligence capabilities to Earth.

While it took us 1000 years longer than Earth did to develop artificial intelligence to the level that you've already reached today after less than 500 years, we have learned some of the precautions that will be necessary in implementing artificial intelligence.

One of the major concerns you should have regarding artificial intelligence applies to my discussion of biases above. Artificial intelligence uses the process of learning from its mistakes in achieving a specific goal or through gathering information available on the World Wide Web.

Unfortunately, since there is no system yet developed to control misinformation on the web, there is even less control over biases. Artificial intelligence will use information that it finds as facts and desirable when in reality they are not. While it might be an exaggeration, I will use the term that has often been referred to when speaking about computerized information - garbage in garbage out. While we have the best intentions for Earth society, providing you with artificial intelligence may be in fact a Trojan horse.

We on Cronin have not yet decided if we should provide you with this technology. I can't give you any specifics right now because we are still determining what may be a realistic test of Earth society to handle this information.

Regarding all the technology that Cronin could provide to Earth, we have not yet determined if our technology combined with your biases regarding social status and behavior will be a blessing or a curse for Earth. While our fusion technology could be the solution to your coming possible demise because of global warming, in the long run our technology could result in a runaway exploitation of natural resources that will allow your species to overwhelm the Earth's resources and lead to your demise in some other way.

Chapter Seventeen

The President and Neil were meeting in the Oval Office to discuss the challenge posed by Gus in his last transmission. The President spoke first.

"You know, Neil, during the last few months, I have often reflected on the significance of our task, especially during the 29 days when we did not have contact with the Cronin people. Now that we have been presented with our challenge, I have reflected more. I have devoted my life to serving the American people and hope to be remembered for my efforts in this regard.

Taking the perspective of a timeline with cosmic proportions, if we were in a race with Cronin towards some goal of complete understanding of the universe and control of our environment and bodies, and that race was one-mile-long, Cronin would only be about one or two inches in front of us on the starting line. Thus, it could be possible that under different circumstances, our roles could be reversed. Furthermore, given all the potential obstacles for us reaching that final goal, we may never reach it. As you know, the Cronin people are facing their imminent demise. I would like you to take that perspective while we discuss responding to the challenge presented to us by the Cronin society.

Furthermore, I would like you to consider the perspective we gained from seeing our planet from the surface of the moon. We are just a small dot in an almost infinite universe. We are all, for better or worse, partners on Earth in our journey through time. If you look at our space program, we have learned that we can cooperate and achieve great things. However, given our current level of technology, it took the efforts of millions of people and the resources of a great nation like the United States to allow just a few people to escape Earth's gravity and walk on the surface of the moon.

Thus, we should continue to explore our solar system and possibly beyond in the future, but for all intents and purposes, we are trapped here on our little planet, and we must make the best of our situation. From the perspective of the moon, it is not possible to see any borders separating one country from another, primarily because those borders are mostly not physical, but borders constructed in our minds. Over the centuries, these borders have led to conflicts, primarily for resources necessary to advance our way of living. On the other hand, much of what we have been able to accomplish in the exploration of space has been the result of cooperation. It appears that when scientists work together on science, they have a common bond that does not lead to conflict.

Hopefully, in our discussions today, if we take this perspective, we can come to a course of action that will allow us to avoid the potential hazards of using the new technology being offered to us by the Cronin people. Whether the decision of the Cronin people to contact the people of the United States was a coincidence or a thought-out decision, our country has had, on balance, a good approach to using resources for the greater good of society rather than for individuals.

The United States has a unique history. Our founding fathers looked for ways that the resources of this great country could be enjoyed by all rather than taken back to another country, as the Spanish did. Our approach was not perfect; we treated the indigenous people who had been on our continent for tens of thousands of years before we arrived as a problem that must be overcome rather than rightful owners of the land they occupied. On the other hand, they established a government that respected state borders and a system of government that allowed people to recognize their differences to achieve common goals for the greater good of society. That system is now under significant stress.

Neil began to speak. "I am honored and humbled by the fact that the people of Cronin decided that I would be the first contact for human society. I can only assume that their choice reflected their belief that a world of science is better than one of beliefs not based upon science. I believe that if the Cronin people were a world of politics, they would have contacted you directly.

In any case, I am here to make the case for the human species' use of science today and our ability to handle the challenges that may be placed on us by a significant increase in our technological capabilities. As you may know, they question our ability to handle it. I will be the first to admit that we have made mistakes along the way and are currently facing some of our greatest existential challenges because of the use of certain technologies. On the other hand, I would like to make a case for the fact that we have been faced with challenges in the past which we are making significant progress towards solving.

To just mention a few, we learned a few years ago about the use of hydrofluorocarbons causing depletion of the ozone in our atmosphere, which in turn was allowing more ultraviolet radiation to reach the surface of the earth. We have basically eliminated the use of these chemicals, and the hole in the atmosphere is closing. During our rapid industrialization, we polluted our water and the atmosphere with the belief that it was a limitless resource, or in the worst case, it was a limited resource, but it could be exploited for those who chose to. Today we enjoy clean air and cleaner water because of our efforts to regulate and prohibit the use of harmful chemicals and procedures.

I guess what I am saying, in another way, is that we should not dwell on what we have done in the past but what we are trying to achieve in the future. Although even there we do face some challenges where some people are not willing to recognize what is true because of scientific study.

The two most glaring differences among citizens regarding science are the value of vaccinations and the reality of global warming. The anti-vaxxers have turned the issue of vaccination from a question of science to a question of personal independence. Somehow, and I don't understand why, people will deny the efficacy of vaccinations or use anecdotal information to make the decision not to be vaccinated. Since this issue is still fresh in our minds from the COVID-19 Pandemic, vaccination is more than a personal issue when you aim to achieve herd immunity, which not only protects the individual but society. It seems that people will believe certain things despite the evidence. After vaccines were widely available, 98% of the people who were hospitalized with the disease were non-vaccinated people.

It may be a little easier to understand the factors leading to the controversy regarding global warming. I believe a large part of the controversy in this area results from the spread of misinformation. The petroleum industry will definitely suffer significantly as a result of the elimination of its products in transportation and industrial processes.

I raised this example also because it is one of the greatest challenges the human species faces today. It is truly an existential threat. Some people characterize this issue as having to save the planet. Well, the planet will do very well without us if we manage to wipe the human species off the face of the earth. Since petroleum is really stored sunlight that resulted from plants and animals that existed millions of years ago when they grew and thrived in an earlier time, we must find alternative sources of energy. In recent years, significant work has been done to generate renewable resources such as solar panels and wind turbines. However, the greatest promise for energy comes from the process that fuels our sun and creates the sunlight that falls upon the earth, that is fusion technology. When two atoms of hydrogen are combined, they form helium and release energy. This process has been going on for billions of years in our sun and all the stars in the universe.

After this process was discovered to produce military weapons, efforts have been made to get the energy in a controlled process. Literally tens of billions of dollars have been expended in this effort already. While we have made some progress, we have a long way to go on our own. The people from Cronin can provide us with this technology. This alone is enough evidence in my mind that we should accept their technology to solve global warming.

While there might be some threats to the human species further down the road, global warming is an immediate issue where we are close to the point of no return regarding the processes in place that are causing the warming.

Regarding Cronin's concern about the equitable sharing of technology and the misuse of other technologies, these should only be a secondary concern if we can't solve the primary concern with global warming. We must start taking steps to face these challenges well in advance of when they start to be an issue.

In the last century, when the human species became aware of the fact that we are now a global society, it started creating organizations that span national borders. The United Nations and NATO are two of the best examples of efforts in this regard. Both of these organizations still recognize a nation's right to self-determination with regard to the people within its borders but must relinquish some control when actions by individual nations have an impact on global society. I believe that we can look to the experience of such organizations in establishing the structure and procedures that they would follow as a guide to establishing a multinational organization to enable the implementation of technology from Cronin while at the same time regulating the misuse of this technology that would lead to the overall detriment to human society.

The wisdom of our forefathers that established this country with a Senate and the House of Representatives, which allows every state to have equal representation regardless of size but then also have another organization that is based upon the population. Such an organization could work well for the global organization that I am proposing.

The final argument that I would make to the Cronin people regarding sharing their technology is simple: we have to try, even if we fail, because we automatically fail if we don't try. Over the long term, we will meet our demise whether it is from human causes or an act of nature as the Cronin society is facing today. The fossil record indicates the human species at one time came down to almost extinction but somehow recovered. There's evidence in all our DNA. The world is a hostile place. Various life forms have existed on Earth and even the stars come and go. If it wasn't for the death of stars, we wouldn't have the larger atoms required for the building blocks of life since they were created when these stars went through the high temperatures and pressures that resulted in their demise.

"Neil, please share the thoughts we have discussed here with Gus in your next communication to him."

Chapter Eighteen

Neil wrote the following email to Gus:

I had a meeting with our President to discuss the issues raised regarding our capacity to use your technology correctly. A transcript of that meeting is attached. I would like to add the following comments as one scientist to another.

I appreciate your concern that we may not use your technology appropriately and your desire to make sure that society gets the benefit of technology rather than some select group of people. I believe we have a culture that provides for an egalitarian distribution of knowledge and recognizes that this is best for society.

Since living in society became more complex and the education that could be provided by a child's parents was not sufficient to make them productive members of society, public education was established. Education was provided free of charge to the student and was funded by taxes from the community. Since it would be a burden for people as they passed through the stage where they had grown children, it was felt more equitable to tax everyone regardless of the number or age of children in their households through local taxation such as real estate taxes.

This concept was originally just for a grammar school education, then later for high school, and now it involves support at the college level. Today, literacy and the other things that are taught in the public school system are essential for people to be productive parts of society. Thus, an investment in a child's education provides returns to society when they reach adulthood.

Before the age of science, religious organizations provided for the recording of information. Later, the university system was established for research and training people in the more sophisticated areas of knowledge such as physics, chemistry, biology, etc. Today, in our university system, any individual who wants to achieve the level of PhD must do original research as part of their application for their degree. These people may either continue in the university and pass sophisticated information on to students who want to work in various fields of science, or they move into the private sector and continue their research.

Today, the government plays a significant role either directly or indirectly in the development of new technology and its practical application for the benefit of society. There are many ways that this takes place. For example, in areas where the development of new technology is risky or so large that it cannot be undertaken by the private sector, the government will fund research until some basic level of understanding is achieved.

The US space program is a good example. Sending people to the moon was such a large task that the US nation backed this program through public taxation. Even at this stage, while the planning and execution of the overall program was under government control, private vendors provided most of the knowledge and material to accomplish the end objective.

Today, most of the development in rocketry is now developed in the private sector. This private development is possible because the rockets can be used to launch satellites operated by the private sector to provide various services. At the same time, these rockets are still used by the government sector to launch satellites such as weather satellites that still provide government-backed services.

The business of science is a risky area because it involves discovery based upon some intuitive idea of what may be possible. But until the potential science is proved through experimentation and development, the risk for any individual or company must be spread upon society as a whole. In the United States and in other countries with free-market systems, this process involves entrepreneurs making proposals regarding goods and services that they believe may have value to the general population, to investors who are willing to invest in various projects.

New technology can provide significant financial rewards to the developers. Investors are willing to back new ventures even though history has shown that only one out of 10 projects will be viable. On the other hand, the rewards of the one viable project more than offset the losses on the other nine projects that did not prove out.

Government also plays a significant role indirectly with the development of new technologies. For example, the rocketry used to send man to the moon had its beginnings in military efforts to use rocketry to deliver weapons in warfare. Today, our Global Positioning System (GPS) was originally developed by the military to help position equipment and facilities of adversaries accurately to attack them. Today, this technology is widely used by civilian navigation systems, which in turn are used to provide information to providers of goods and services to the people who are using these systems. For example, a person making a trip to another city can use these systems to locate restaurants, hotels, and other service providers, based upon their location.

The combination of cellular services and global positioning systems has had more impact on society and economic development than any other development since the age of science started.

The military also supports the development of civilian activities indirectly. For example, pilots who have been trained to fly military aircraft can become pilots in civilian aviation at significantly less cost than if they had to start their training from scratch, rather than building upon the know-how and skills that they acquired in the military.

After several decades of efforts and expenditures to develop fusion technology to produce electricity, we are now at an inflection point. In December of 2020, for the first time ever, a fusion technology facility was able to generate 50% more power than the power used to start the fusion reaction. Now that commercial development of fusion technology is projected within the next 5 to 10 years, the private sector is again getting into this area for the commercial exploitation of the technology.

There are now over 50 firms that have raised investor funds ranging from over $700 million to just $10 million. As we have discussed, your sharing of your technology in fusion technology is one of the best places to start. Now that the industry is being established, it can be the vehicle by which your technology is implemented. It will significantly accelerate the implementation of this technology and reduce the risks associated with it.

The implementation of fusion technology has great significance for our planet. Even without global warming, the ability to produce significant low-cost energy will have a great benefit for global society on Earth. Since fusion technology is carbon-free, it can be the technology that will address the existential threat of rising sea levels and climate change presented to the human species.

I hope that you can agree with the points I make here. I know that you are reluctant to provide your technology to Earth if it could not be implemented in a way that agreed with the values of Cronin society. Unfortunately, we are presented with a significant dilemma. There's no way that

Human Society could prove to you that we are worthy of receiving your technology in the short time that Cronin society has. Now that I have described how we develop technology on Earth and how it eventually benefits society on an egalitarian basis, I hope this is not that different from what your experience has been over the years since you entered the age of technology.

I would be interested to know if Cronin society followed some of the same practices and social values that we have on Earth. It would go a long way for our understanding about what is the same throughout the universe. We both know that physics and chemistry are the same throughout the vast universe. Intuitively, I believe maybe even the social behavior that intelligent beings engage in is somehow based on some basic part of the fabric of the universe.

If that can be determined by comparing our two societies, that could be the greatest legacy of your contact with Earth. The practical application of your technology could move forward with the hopeful understanding that there is significantly more order in the universe than we ever anticipated.

Within a few hours, Gus responded:

"Neil, thank you for your concise summary of how Earth engages in science discovery, technology development, and the ultimate implementation of that technology for the betterment of your society. I can tell you that Cronin society follows very similar procedures and social values regarding scientific discovery and the implementation of that information for the benefit of our society.

As a person of science, I have an unbelievable sense of wonder of what we have learned about consistency throughout the universe. We knew that it was true regarding physics because we could use the history of light technology to tell us what was true about stars and planets vast distances away from our own planet. However, to be able to determine how extensive this consistency was, it was necessary for our two planets to encounter each other and share their collective experience. As we both know, there are many planets like ours that can support intelligent life spread around the vast universe; some civilizations have already come and gone, others have yet to be born.

We know that it makes sense that the physics of stars and planets throughout the universe should be consistent since they all sprang from a singularity billions of years ago. On the other hand, the development of intelligent life on individual planets, which have no connection with each other as intelligent life is developing, makes me believe some greater order in the universe exists to allow such a development to happen.

Since we appear to be traveling along the same road where we are a few miles down the road ahead of you, our successful implementation of technology, which we are sharing with you, makes me believe that order in the universe will allow you to avoid any pitfalls that may arise either anticipated or unanticipated. This understanding makes me very hopeful for any intelligent life on other planets that we have not discovered will progress accordingly.

With this new insight, we have decided to go forward with sharing our entire database of information with Earth. We only have a short time before the demise of our planet, but as I have told you already, we have built up a legacy arc of everything relating to our history and the technology that we have developed.

This arc will be manned by several individuals who are caretakers of our legacy. They have established protocols which will allow the orderly download of our information to Earth. While these individuals can assist you in your process of downloading the information, the system is fully automated and should allow you to accomplish the download within a time frame that will be much shorter than any anticipated malfunctions in our arc.

With all this being said, you know we face our demise due to what could best be described as the random motion of a large asteroid intersecting with the orbital path of our planet. Thus, it could be said that considering all the consistency within the universe regarding physical matter, there is still a significant random aspect in our universe. I guess that future generations or future civilizations maybe someday be able to uncover some secret that removes even this random aspect of the universe. Maybe creation and destruction are a part of the natural order of things.

Unfortunately, I cannot think of a way that we could subject this hypothesis to a scientific method experiment. In any case, it adds to my wonder that I couldn't even speculate about such a phenomenon. I guess this question fits in with other questions such as can intelligent life ever have enough intelligence to understand itself"

"The Final Chapter"

The following is Neil's last email to Gus:

"So, my friend, what have we learned from our brief encounter? It appears that life develops similarly in separate parts of the universe that we know are not connected. On the other hand, the comparison of life on two planets confirms what we might intuitively assume to be correct, since we all come from a common source if we go back far enough.

We learned that life occurs in cycles, as an accommodation to changes in environmental conditions, but also because of changes in the social order of intelligent beings. We determined that if life developed on two planets in a very small part of the huge universe, life must exist throughout the universe. Some of that life is intelligent life that has developed a social order to enhance its continuation. Due to the vast distances that separate planets providing certain sets of conditions conducive to the development of life, most life lives in isolation from other life forms.

We have learned that the cycle of life is very short relative to the time cycles that govern the physical universe. Ironically, we use cycles in the physical universe to measure life. Life exists as so many revolutions of a planet or orbits of that planet around the sun.

The universe does not express a preference for one life form over another. In fact, animals get their energy to exist and move about from energy stored up in other animals or plants. While nature creates life, it also destroys it on a regular basis through the destructive force of the encounter of celestial objects. On a much smaller scale, because of microbes living off their host until they consume the host, and in the process, destroying themselves.

Through the ages of intelligent life, there has been a conflict between religion and science as to which provides the current explanation for life and its purpose. On the other hand, both rely on some higher authority. Religion calls this God, and science calls it nature. While scientists consider themselves superior to religious leaders in providing explanations for natural phenomena, even scientists eventually reach unknown areas, such as where did the universe come from before it exploded from a singularity to the vast universe we know today. Also, science has yet to explain how the very first steps of life occur. While the citizens of Cronin have been engaged in the process of science for thousands of years longer than the citizens of Earth, they still have many unanswered questions, some of which may never be answered with the tools or capacities of intelligent life.

Our contact has revealed differences between our overall philosophies of Earth versus that of Cronin society. The human species has assumed that it is somewhat superior and apart from all other life on their planet. Thus, they can exploit the resources, both living and nonliving, however they wish. This hubris leads humans to believe that no matter what they do, their intelligence and science can overcome these limitations.

Furthermore, the citizens of Earth believe that intelligent life has no end or at least no end until it is overcome by physical phenomena in the universe that are so great that they cannot control them. The people of Cronin, on the other hand, determined many years ago that intelligent life on Cronin was an integral part of the natural order and must behave accordingly.

Ironically, as citizens of Cronin have reached the limit of intelligent life, it will be annihilated by a phenomenon in the physical universe that it cannot control. The fact that the Cronin society developed a science project that eventually led to contact with Earth reveals that an important part of life is emotions. The fact that intelligent life can be inspired by wonder and curiosity to learn what we can about how things work, how to make things better for the quality of life, and whether other beings exist besides those that inhabit our small corner of the universe.

What the people of Earth and Cronin have discovered about the vastness and complexity of the universe is a very humbling experience, certainly for any one individual but also for society. I believe that humility is a significant factor in the quality of life. What we can accomplish as an individual is very dependent upon the efforts of those who went before us, and the grace of intelligence bestowed upon us by the universe."

It was November 1st. Ironically, it was also All Saints' Day. In the Roman Catholic Church and other Christian churches, All Saints' Day is a day established by the Pope over 1200 years ago to commemorate all Saints, both known and unknown. It was also less than 48 hours until an asteroid would impact Cronin and smash it out of existence.

"Gus, I know this is a difficult time for you, but I wanted to take a few minutes to reflect on our encounter over the last few months. Also attached to this communication is a compilation of comments from most of the heads of state on our planet. A few countries, for whatever reason, chose not to have comments included in this message.

In our culture, we have funeral services for people who have passed. These ceremonies are more for the living than the person who passed. After some time has passed, sometimes years and sometimes never, people will evaluate the impact that a person had while they were alive. Our encounter was between two intelligent life forms that had the good fortune to encounter each other. Although this was most likely just fate, it will be one of the most significant accomplishments in the universe. While our encounter is the only one that we know about, there may have been others, or will be others that occur in the universe, since it's so vast with literally billions of stars and trillions of planets. But even then, our encounter is significantly rare.

The nature of life is such that it has a beginning and an end and compared to the existence of inanimate material, the lifespan is but a flash in the timeline of the universe. All living things have at least one purpose: to be born, mature, reproduce, and raise their offspring until they are able to reproduce and continue the cycle. This cycle can be a matter of days or more than 100 years. Beyond participating in their reproductive cycle, an individual's existence, no matter how long, is measured in what impact they can have on the world that they lived in. By this measure, you are truly unique since you not only impacted your own culture but have had a long-lasting impact upon the people of Earth. Personally, I want to thank you for that contribution and tell you that our short encounter will be the most significant event in my life. Somehow, I feel that these mere words cannot convey the deep gratitude that I have for your efforts to reach out to the people of Earth.

Few people are fortunate enough or unfortunate enough to know the time and place of their ultimate demise. I can only imagine the emotions you were feeling at this time. However, whatever life you and the people of Cronin may have after the impact of the asteroid, I wish you all the best."

After about 8 hours, Gus returned with the following message:

"Neil, thank you for your good wishes and gratitude. As I face my demise, I consider myself a very, very lucky person. We all want to live as long as possible but realize that there is an end so we live our life every day with the thought that we make as much of an impact as we can while we are here.

As you know, our mission to planet Earth was launched with the knowledge that it would take 41 years for our probe to reach your planet and then an unknown number of years studying your planet to determine if or ever, we would contact you. Even though our lifespan on Cronin is a little longer than yours on Earth, my efforts as the leader of the program to contact Earth encompassed most of my life, especially when you consider the time I spent working to be appointed the head of the program. While we are both people of science, we recognize that fate or the universe, if you prefer to call it that, plays a very significant part in our lives. Although the time from when we launched our project to send the probe was very long in terms of an individual's lifespan, it was insignificant in terms of the history of the universe. Despite that, at any point in those fifty-plus years, many things could have happened that would result in the failure of our mission. How ironic would it have been that two intelligent societies who discovered each other's existence and tried to have contact would have had that effort ended by some chance factor such as an equipment malfunction or encounter with other celestial objects such as an asteroid.

With all that, I was able to accomplish my life's ambition, which was truly monumental. While I had hoped that I might have had the opportunity to see how our technology transfer and exchange of other information had impacted life on Earth, I feel that I have lived a life very worth living, and I am at peace with events that will unfold in the next few hours.

I would like to conclude with your Irish proverb:

'May the road rise up to meet you.

May the wind always be at your back.

May the sunshine be warm upon your face, and rains fall soft upon your fields.

And until we meet again, May God hold you in the palm of his hand.'

Hours later, Neil received an email from Gus with these three words:

'Farewell, my friend.'

35 years later, telescopes on Earth will detect a brief and faint flash of light from the region in the sky where Cronin once was.

About the Author: The author enjoys a lifelong interest in astronomy and science in general since his first visit to the Hayden Planetarium at the American Museum of Natural History. For a major part of his working career, he has evaluated new technology and the products and services that have used these technologies. Some of these technologies include microcomputers, cellular telephones, and electronic payment systems. He has authored over 100 articles and book-length reports on microcomputer software, telecommunication products and services, and financial payment systems. In addition to his consulting company, he has worked for several Fortune 500 companies and has also engaged in two entrepreneurial ventures. He is a native New Yorker and now lives in New Jersey."

Printed in Dunstable, United Kingdom

71330528R00133